M000215069

# EVERY DUKE
# HAS A
# SILVER LINING

TAMARA

# COPYRIGHT

Every Duke has a Silver Lining
The Wayward Woodvilles, Book 4
Copyright © 2022 by Tamara Gill
Cover Art by Wicked Smart Designs
Editor Grace Bradley Editing, LLC

This book is a work of fiction. The names, characters, places, and incidents are products of the writer's imagination or have been used fictitiously and are not to be construed as real. Any resemblance to persons, living or dead, actual events, locales or organizations is entirely coincidental.

All rights reserved. Without limiting the rights under copyright reserved above, no part of this publication may be reproduced, stored in or introduced into a database and retrieval system or transmitted in any form or any means (electronic, mechanical, photocopying, recording or otherwise) without the prior written permission of both the owner of copyright and the above publishers.

ISBN: 978-0-6454177-9-1

# CHAPTER
# ONE

*London Season, 1808*

Ashley glanced out the carriage window and frowned, her stomach in knots, her head spinning over what she was supposed to do. She glanced back at her friends seated across from her, their wide, laughing eyes no support or help.

"I cannot do this. What if I'm caught! If any gentleman who knows my family or recognizes me tells, I'll be ruined."

"You lost the bet," Anna stated, throwing her a disapproving look. Her closest friend in London, Lady Anna, was always up to no good and seemed to get away with it more often than not. Probably because she was an earl's daughter, and no one suspected the lady to be as wicked as she was.

But Lady Anna was not so innocent, and this bet that Ashley lost to her was proof of that. The task was impossible, not to mention dangerous.

She groaned, looking out onto the darkened street again, seeing several gentlemen enter the premises several

1

houses down the dark lane. A gentleman's gaming club, or supposedly it was, so Anna stated, but Ashley was not so sure. Several women of dubious employment had entered while they had been stationed here, and she was starting to think it was more than a place for men to lose their money.

Their virginity, too, for those who had it to lose.

"If you go around the back, there will be an entrance. My brother told me so during one of his nights of revelry when he was still in his cups and told me all he got up to." Anna laughed. "Upstairs, you will find the office and subsequent desk of Grady Kolten. The bastard Duke of Blackhaven, or he will be when he inherits from his father."

The name sounded as ominous as this dare. "All you need to do is take his quill, and you would have done what we all promised should any of us have lost the bet. Which," she said, raising her brow and looking down her straight nose at her, "you indeed did."

"I do not believe our little bet on cards is worth my reputation. If he catches me, he could drag me back to Mayfair by the ear and throw me before the duke. Or worse, demand my brother-in-law hand over blunt to release me. There are a million ways this could go wrong."

Ashley chewed the end of her glove, reconsidering this night and her three friends who would make her do such a thing. How she wished her best friend from Grafton was in town. Daphne would know what to do.

"Do not spoil the evening," Paisley whined. "I had to steal the quill from Lady Jenkin's desk, and it had a golden tip. No doubt she will be missing it and will demand answers from her staff."

"Maybe you ought to return that," Caroline interjected. "We do not want to take anything of value from these people. Especially since this is only a game."

"Come now, Ashley. Go about the back, run upstairs, grab the quill, and be done with it. You will be in and out in five minutes, and we will not leave without you. All will be well, trust me," Anna said, her smile all innocence.

Ashley sighed, slipping the hood from her domino over her head and jumping from the carriage. Her silk slippers dampened, and she glanced down. The unmentionable puddle made her evening merely more revolting.

Slamming the carriage door and glaring at her friends, she turned and started down the lane that ran beside the gaming hell. Coming to the yard, she could see many empty wooden pallets stacked neatly around the fence. Empty wine and beer bottles stacked in neat piles. They certainly went through a lot of beverages at this venue.

She kept to the shadows as much as she could before she came to a solid-wood door. Pushing on it, she prayed it was locked, and her excursion would be over, but surprisingly it was not. It creaked, the sound like a drum as it slowly swung open before she slipped through and into the hell.

The sound of men laughing, shouts of betting on the gaming tables, and music floated through the building, but far enough away that she hoped she would not be seen. The corridor was long, and halfway down, a staircase led to the second floor. Checking she was alone, she started up the stairs and came to the top to find another corridor with rooms leading off it.

Which one would be this Grady Kolten's office? For a moment, she stood there, unsure which direction to turn, before taking a guess and heading left.

The upstairs was eerily quiet, and her stomach roiled with nerves. What would she do if anyone caught her?

What would she do if the person who did find her snooping about was dangerous and caused her harm?

She stilled as a creaking board sounded behind her, and was about to flee from this nightmare of her own making when the startling cold press of metal against her neck halted even her heart.

*Oh dear God, I am going to die.*

"Looking for something?" a deep, gravelly voice whispered against her ear. She dared not move as the pinch of the blade stung. Had he cut her? How would she explain the mark to her family? If she ever saw them again, that was.

"I'm sorry, sir. I meant no harm. It was merely a lark—a bet. I should not be here. I should not have come," she babbled, closing her mouth to halt the panic she heard in her voice.

"Hmm," he said, taking the knife from her throat and hoisting her over his shoulder as if she weighed no more than a flour sack. He strode into a room with one window, a large desk, and several walls of shelving and slammed the door closed on her escape. Ashley sent up a final prayer to the heavens to try to get her out of this predicament. She should never have listened to her friends. She should never have come. And now, she would die in the cesspit of East London, and her family would never know why.

G rady slipped the featherlight woman off his shoulder, ignoring the sweet ass he'd gripped to hold her steady, and threw her onto the daybed, which sat beneath his office window.

He stood back, staring down at the miss, and cursed. She was a lady. The diamond earbobs told him that, if the perfectly unblemished skin and clear eyes did not. He took a calming breath, not needing such a distraction. Not tonight, in any case. He had a gaming hell to run, a life to lead. A mistress to bed. He did not need this young miss messing up his debauched plans.

"What are you doing prying about my hell? Do you even know where you are, Miss..." he asked, hoping she would give him her name.

She raised her chin, setting her hood off her head to sit on her shoulders. She patted at her dark-brown hair, checking the curls were in place while watching him with eyes that were too wide, too perfect to be true.

Damn, the idiot chit was pretty.

"I'm Ashley, and what I said upon meeting you, sir, was true. I'm here only as a lark, a game with my friends. I lost a bet, so I was sent on a mission to steal the quill off your desk. I see now the error of my way, so if you'll excuse me, I shall be going now."

She stood and went to step past him, and Grady clasped her shoulders, pushing her back onto the daybed, not quite ready to let her leave. It had been some time since he had been around such a beautiful woman of rank. He narrowed his eyes, wondering who she really was. She was not just Ashley nobody.

"And your surname, so I may inform your family of your wayward antics here this evening?"

Her eyes flew wide, and she strode over to him, taking his hands and squeezing them with more strength than he thought her capable of. "Oh no, you cannot tell my family. I will be sent home, and I'm so enjoying the Season so far. I have many suitors, and although they're as young as me, some are nice and have potential. If I'm sent home, I shall have no options for a husband, and that will never do."

Grady's lips twitched, and he cleared his throat,

reminding himself that this was not an amusing situation. "You could have been raped and murdered in this part of London. Do you know how dangerous it is for a woman of your position to have snuck into a gaming hell? This could have been a dwelling of ill repute, and you could, right at this moment, be under a man who would have your skirts lifted, taking his fill. Did you think of that, *Ashley*?" he asked her, ignoring the pang of guilt as she flinched at his words.

He meant to be cruel. She ought to realize how dangerous her being here was. The silly little fool could have lived her last night on earth, not merely London. She could have ended up floating facedown in the Thames.

And now he had to decide what to do with her, so she did not.

# TWO

Ashley stared up at the behemoth of a man who she assumed was Grady Kolten, but her friend had mentioned him as being the bastard Duke of Blackhaven? He was a gentleman then, and surely that would mean a little of his breeding would keep him from hurting her.

"Are you truly the future Duke of Blackhaven?" she asked him, her attention snapping to his uncouth dressing habits. The man was an enigma. He certainly did not look like a gentleman. His hair was in need of a good trim, and there was a distinct shadowing of stubble on his jaw. Not to mention his clothing. While clean and respectable, it was certainly not cut from the best tailor in London, but still, his breeches did fit and hug his form very well.

The man was devastatingly handsome but gave off an air of danger in all truth. A man who ought never to be crossed—the small scar across his left cheekbone proof of that.

While he may be born noble, she did not think he had always acted so. She gained the impression that no matter how angry he was at her being here or how annoying her presence, he would not hurt her. He may scold her, and deservedly so, but nothing more.

He frowned, and she got a glimpse of the hardness of the fellow, a man who made his living in the seedier sides of London and did not take fools lightly.

"I'm not a duke *yet*," he said, rubbing his jaw, the sound of stubble being stroked all she could hear.

"You do not attend the Season?" she asked him, hoping just a little that the overbearing, foreboding, and utterly devastating gentleman before her may scuff the boards during her coming-out year. He would certainly make the otherwise mundane Season gain a little levity.

He threw back his head and bellowed in laughter. She sighed, not needing him to answer to tell her what he thought of that notion.

Ashley looked about the room, surprised now that she was right-side up how comfortable and opulent the space was. Nothing like she had assumed upon first arriving there. She had thought it would be drafty, without comforts, and hard like the man himself.

She waited for his amusement to subside before she would bother to ask him any more questions.

"Come, you're leaving, and if I see you wandering the halls of this hell again, you will not like the punishment, Ashley," he said, pulling her toward the door.

She wrenched from his hold, lifting her chin. "I can leave without your assistance. I have a carriage waiting."

He raised his brow, striding to the door and ripping the greatcoat off the brass hook, slipping his muscular arms through the coat and distracting her a moment.

Ashley licked her parched lips.

She followed him and ignored the fact he did not wait

for her but merely believed she would follow him like a puppy. The man was infuriating. What future duke did not know proper manners toward a lady? Even one who lived most of his time in gaming hells.

"If you're to be a duke, what are you now? Do not men of your ilk have a courtesy title until they come into their inheritance?"

His shoulders stiffened, and he shook his head. "You're very meddling for a debutante. Is this why you're not yet married? No husband willing to put up with your incessant chatter? It grates on my ears, if you want any sort of truth."

Never in her life had she been spoken to with such little respect, and she glared at his back. "You're very rude, my lord as well," she said. "I was merely trying to start a conversation."

He scoffed, starting down the stairs. "Tell me who you are, Ashley, and I may be truthful in turn. Not that I do not have an inkling..."

"Inkling, my lord. Please enlighten me," she said.

He stopped on the stairs, turning, and his height, even two steps before her, made him still higher than herself. Her mind blanked as to what they were talking of for a moment. She stopped, almost colliding with his chest. This close to him, the scent of sandalwood and lavender teased her senses. Her attention snapped to his lips, full and mocking as he stared at her.

Ashley swallowed, the pit of her stomach twisting into delicious knots. Who was this man? So mysterious, dark, and foreboding. How could a lady not be affected?

"A duke's daughter or some peer of the realm, I would guess. A woman used to getting everything she wishes without a thought to others. Your little escapade here this evening reeks of privilege and stupidity. The thought you're invincible, and nothing bad will happen to you because of who you are. Am I right?"

Ashley gaped before shutting her mouth with a snap and glaring at him for the hundredth time. The man was impossible. "I'm not nobility like you, my lord. My father is a gentleman, gentry, but not titled. Growing up with my four sisters, I shared a maid and knew all the servants by name at my parents' home. I do not think the same could be said of you, future duke," she said, knowing her use of the title was incorrect but wanting to make a point of it in any case. Especially since the man refused to tell her his current title and who he was known by now.

Something flickered in his green eyes, respect perhaps, but certainly disapproval. "I had no servants growing up, so it seems we're both wrong, in a way," he added as if an afterthought.

Ashley said not another word, merely followed him out the back of the hell where the empty pallets of beverages sat. "Where to now?" she asked him. "Are you going to let me leave?"

He clasped her arm, dragging her along the shadowy lane. "No. I'm taking you home, and I'll tell your family what you did this evening. They will know what to do with a hellion like you."

Ashley's heart faltered. No, she would not be sent home. The heathen would not get away with this. This was her time in London, and she'd be damned if she would miss it simply because she bested him and his pathetic security at the hell.

"The hell you will," she said, wrenching his hold on her before she ran as if the devil himself were after her. Which she wasn't certain was not the case.

# THREE

Grady allowed her to think she had escaped before with a few quick steps, he hoisted her over his shoulder for a second time. He strode to the carriage that waited at the top of the lane, three pairs of wide, fearing eyes stared at him as he made his way toward them.

The driver tipped his hat to Grady, and he nodded in reply. "Mayfair if you please," he said, opening the carriage door. He hoisted Ashley inside the carriage, ignoring her gasp of offense when his hand slid down her leg. He followed close behind, sitting beside her, more than aware of her presence.

He took a calming breath, wrenching his greatcoat into place and ignoring his body's response to the menacing chit.

"You three," he growled, taking in the three women looking at him as if he were about to chop off their heads from their swanlike necks. "Where in Mayfair do you reside? I will see each of you home and hope that I do not see you here again. I will not be so accommodating next time."

The three girls nodded, mumbling their addresses—all but one. Ashley remained mulish and quiet at his side. Her presence made his skin prickle in awareness, and his idea to see her home now seemed a foolish error.

The scent of jasmine wafted in the vehicle, and he breathed deep. So long since he had smelled such sweet air. His hell often reeked of sweat and sex when his customers made use of the ladies who plied their trade behind his doors.

But inside the equipage, the sweet scent made him long for things he'd given up hoping for many years ago. One by one, Grady called out the lady's addresses to the driver and saw them safely to their homes.

He sat across from Ashley on Charles Street in Mayfair at a standstill as she continued to refuse to tell him where she lived.

"For the final time, where do you live, Ashley? I want the address. Now," he demanded, losing patience fast—the menacing chit pushed him beyond his endurance.

He could not blame her. His telling her parents of her whereabouts would not end well for her, and she probably would be sent back to the country to learn proper etiquette.

Grady ground his teeth at the thought of her rusticating so far away from the city. He resented the feeling it wrought inside him more than anything else.

"Please, you cannot tell anyone what I did tonight. I will be sent away, and my chance at finding a love match as my sisters have will be over. Please, just take me home but do not confront my family. I promise to behave, and I will not participate in any more dares."

The words that she would behave sent a bolt of lust

through him. She was already naughty, and he could make her more so with instruction. The idea had merit, but he would not entertain it further. He did not have time for an innocent debutante. Not when he had a mistress he could fuck whenever he wished, no other strings attached to that arrangement.

He mulled over her words, pushing down the guilt her beseeching gaze wrought on his conscience. "If I allow you to return home, you will swear to me that you'll never do such an idiotic thing again. No matter if you lose friends over that promise."

She nodded, several brown locks falling from their pins and pooling about her shoulders. His gaze dipped to her neck, the silk gown accentuating her ample bosom and small waist.

The chit ought to be betrothed already. What was wrong with men that they did not want what was sitting before them? She was so very lovely, elegant and smart. Her opinions given with just the right amount of fervor.

His lips twitched. She had certainly made his otherwise boring evening a little more lively.

"I promise, my lord. I shall never do such an idiotic thing again." She threw him a sweet smile, and he narrowed his eyes, wondering if she meant what she said or if she were merely stating what he wanted to hear so she could be let free. To have another night to cause mischief across the city.

"Very well," he relented, leaning back into the squabs. "And now you will tell me where you live and who your parents are so I may know whom to inform should I see you out of the respectable areas of London once again."

"The Duke of Derby's residence, Berkeley Square," she called out to the hackney cab driver. The flick of the whip and the carriage jerking forward pulled Grady from his shock.

"How are you related to Derby?" he asked, having not expected that response from her, not after their earlier conversation back at the hell.

She looked down her nose at him, stating without words what she thought of his question. "Derby is my brother-in-law. He married my older sister, Hailey." She crossed her arms, the action accentuating her breasts. He so did not need the distraction. She had already diverted him enough.

"Really? So that would make you one of the Woodville sisters overtaking London. You are talked about even in my hell, which is not common. But all the more reason to keep out of it going forward or pay the price."

The carriage turned a corner, and she reached up, clasping the straps above the window with her gloved hand. "If our family is discussed, it is only good things, I'm sure. We're not scandalous like some people I've been unfortunate enough to meet."

He scoffed, unable to tear his eyes from her just as the carriage rocked to a halt before one of London's grandest homes. "Do not let me see you again, Miss Woodville," he said, opening the door and gesturing for her to leave.

She wiggled forward on her seat, reaching into her pocket. Grady felt his mouth gape at the sight of what she held. A new quill waved before his face—his quill—and the little minx had the audacity to tickle his nose. She laughed, jumping from the equipage before he could reach for it.

"Good night, my lord, and thank you for your discretion. I look forward to not seeing you again too." She smirked, starting through the gates and toward the front door of the grand house. "Thank you for the quill," she called over her shoulder. "I never like to lose a dare, and I have not yet. Not even tonight."

Grady found himself smiling. He tried to school his features, be disapproving of her antics, but could not. How could anyone be anything but charmed by the chit? As maddening as she was.

He yelled out directions to the driver, glad when she disappeared from view. He took a deep breath, looking but not seeing Mayfair as it gave way to the East End. All he could envision was a brown-haired chit with a wicked sense of fun and a mouth made for sin.

If only he were still a gentleman, maybe she would have given him cause to attend a Season. Unfortunately, he was not.

L ater that night, Ashley lay in bed, staring up at the darkened ceiling, the feel of the quill against her face soothing her to sleep. This evening had been one of the most invigorating, terrifying at times, night of her life.

Meeting Grady Kolten had been an unexpected gift. He was coarse, mouthy, and had little trouble telling her his opinions, but his handsomeness made all other cons skulk into the background.

She closed her eyes, picturing him. What a shame he would not attend the Season's entertainments. Unless...

She sat up, excitement thrumming through her veins.

Her coming-out ball was a week away, and there was still time for invitations to be sent. What a lark if she were to invite him. Would he come? She doubted he would, but she could imagine his amusement at her inviting him.

He would know she was thinking of him and their time together, which she was. He had occupied her mind constantly since he departed several hours ago, and she did not think she would stop thinking of him for some time to come.

Ashley sighed, flopping back onto her bedding. If only he were a gentleman, their interludes would not have to stop. Either that, or she'd go back on her word and seek him out once more at his hell.

Would he scold her again? Become flushed and furious, of high color, and devastatingly handsome like this evening?

That plan had merit. He was not her guardian or parent after all. Very high-handed of him to demand her to do anything he said. He was not her boss, and mayhap he needed a reminder of that fact.

And soon.

# FOUR

G rady walked through the gambling tables of his hell, stopping to watch the gentlemen try their luck against the house, which, fortunately for him, was often unsuccessful.

A shame he could not say the same for himself in his personal life. The past week had been less than satisfactory, and he knew the reason as to why. Reflections of a certain brown-haired minx invaded his dreams and made his sleep almost impossible. Not to mention he found himself staring at nothing at all and thinking of her quick wit at the most inconvenient times.

He had woken several nights, hard and hot, sweat pouring off him in spades. The chit haunted his every hour, and even now, watching his club make more money than most men dream of in a lifetime, all he could think of was her.

Miss Ashley Woodville.

The *ton's* darling, or so he had been able to garner from visiting Whites earlier this week for the first time in years,

which had caused quite a stir and many calls for celebration.

Not that he was back in society or had any intention of
attending the entertainments this Season. He merely
wanted to hear what tidbit of news he could garner, and if
any of that information involved Ashley Woodville, all the
better.

He strolled by a table of gamblers and noted the players,
one, in particular, Cedrik Marabel, the Earl of Walsh. The
hairs on the back of his neck stood on end at the sight of the
man. Like his father the Marquess of Gibson, Lord Walsh
was cut from the same filthy cloth and it was worth keeping
him in check.

His words with Viscount Fenton floated to him and his
steps faltered, so he could listen further.

"Are you attending the Woodville chit's coming-out
ball? It's tonight and sure to be an event of the Season since
Derby is hosting," Lord Walsh stated, throwing more blunt
onto the table without apprehension.

Lord Fenton nodded, sipping his whisky and kneading
the breast of a whore who sat on his lap, wiggling enthusi-
astically. "I am, headed there next. I thought I might try to
court Lady Anna Bell. She's rich as Croesus and pretty
enough."

"Too true," Lord Walsh stated, reaching out to touch
Suzie's nipple and eliciting a giggle from her. "But I want
Miss Woodville herself. What a fine piece of ass. I tried to
scurry her away at a ball the other evening, but she would
not have it. Told me to bugger off if you do not mind." Lord
Walsh smirked. "Made me want her all the more, and
Father has approved of the match. She's an heiress, you
know. Richer than most of the ladies in the *ton*."

Grady relaxed his hands at his sides, refusing to get into

fisticuffs with either gentleman. He was not so pure and perfect to call them out on their actions or speech. Even so, the thought of Miss Woodville going anywhere near Lord Walsh or becoming his wife made his blood run cold. To be near Lord Walsh meant she would be near his father, the Marquess of Gibson. Over his dead body, would he allow such a thing.

"We should probably finish up here and head off soon. I do not want to miss our time courting the ladies. I doubt either one will be on the marriage mart next Season, and we must make our moves while we can."

"Too true," Lord Fenton stated, downing his wine. "But first, should we escort Suzie upstairs? Quell the fire between our legs before dancing with the respectable misses. Do not want a cockstand getting in between our future brides and us, now do we?"

Lord Walsh laughed, dipping his hand between Suzie's legs. Her groan and hastening to stand telling of her approval.

Grady stood to the side, watching them leave, and thought about what he should do. Several days ago, he had received an invitation to Miss Ashley Woodville's coming-out ball on Berkeley Square. To his disgust, he had lifted the expensive parchment to his nose, if only to see if the paper smelled of jasmine, just like Ashley did.

It had not, yet he wondered if she had penned the invitation herself. Was the invite a tease, a taunt to see if he would rise to her bait and attend?

He had intended to ignore it, but now he was not so sure he should. Not with the likes of Lord Walsh and Fenton being in attendance.

. . .

Ashley stood at the side of the room, her three sisters, all titled, married ladies, beside her and watching over her like matrons protecting their chick from the rakes of the *ton*.

Little did they know she had met the worst of what society had to offer, and she found him utterly charming. Not that she knew who he was at first, but her friend Lady Anna Bell had soon informed her of his aristocratic ties.

Grady Kolten, Earl of Howley, was not who she expected to meet when she snuck into his gaming hell. A stroke of luck if she were honest with herself. To be caught could have been so much worse had the man not been a gentleman at all.

She smiled and greeted those who came through the receiving line. Tonight was her coming-out ball, a celebration her family had planned for weeks. She, too, had been looking forward to the evening, but the night would be more exciting if one invitation, in particular, were accepted.

Would he attend? Would he come and shock the *ton* with his reappearance?

Ashley sighed, knowing her wish was just that. A dream that would not come true. He had told her to behave and not return to his club, and she had not. Their little excursion to the East End seemed to have scared her friends into behaving more like the ladies they were born to be, and none of them had participated in another dare since.

Ashley spied her friend Anna being asked to dance by Lord Fenton, and she frowned. She did not like the man even though he was Lord Walsh's good friend. There was something off about his lordship, as if he were one not to be trusted.

"I see Lord Walsh is here this evening and looking very

handsome indeed," her sister Isla noted, nodding in the direction his lordship stood with several gentlemen.

"I see too," Ashley said, watching his lordship. He was nice enough, she supposed, always kind and considerate to her. But he could pick better friends. Whenever he was around Lord Fenton, she had the impression he wanted to please and do whatever the viscount wished.

"Maybe keep a dance for his lordship free since he is a particular favorite of yours," Isla mentioned, giving her a small smile.

"I do not have favorites, sisters. Do not play match-maker, if you will. Just because you all found love in your first Season does not mean I will, and you know that I will not accept anything less. Even if that means that I do not marry for two or three Seasons."

Hailey smiled. "I do not think you will find it difficult to find love. There is a man out in the *ton* with your name on him. He merely needs to make himself known."

The master of ceremonies called out the next guest to arrive, and Ashley's heart landed in her mouth. Her attention flew to the doors, and heat spread from her cheeks to her neck. She dared not look down, knowing she would be splotchy and red.

Her attention snapped to Anna, and she could read the fear on her friend's visage and knew it was a mirror image of hers.

What was he doing here?

Had he come after all?

She swallowed, cursing herself a fool. She had invited him here, that was why. But what would he do now that he was here? She really should have thought more on the subject before bringing a man who could ruin her and cause strife with her family should he utter a word of her dare. Would he seek out her family and tell them what she had done? Where she had traveled to? What she had stolen?

As if her riling thoughts of him summoned his attention, his eyes met hers across the sea of heads, and she fought to breathe, her heart beating a thousand drums in her ears.

"Who is that, Ashley?" Hailey asked her. Ashley could hear the uncertainness in her eldest sister's voice.

Understandable, too, since Lord Howley was dressed in black, not an ounce of white clothing on him anywhere. Not even his shirt or cravat. Everything he wore was as black as night.

Or as black as his soul...

Ashley knew this was not so, no matter what reputation he may have. He had not treated her unkindly when he found her.

*He had held a knife to your neck...*

She shook the thought aside, the pit of her stomach twisting into knots when he started toward her, his height placing him above most of those in attendance.

It was like the devil himself was coming to collect her, gain his payment for her dealings with him, and she was powerless to stop him.

Not that she wished to stop him at all.

# CHAPTER
# FIVE

Grady ignored the murmurings that accompanied his every step as he found his quarry and made his way toward her.

Miss Woodville looked like a woman about to face the guillotine, and he fought back his grin, knowing she had not expected him to attend this evening.

He bowed before her and her three sisters, all of whom were as pretty as the youngest, standing in front of them like a prized jewel ready for the taking.

"Miss Woodville, thank you for the invitation. I hope your ball has been enjoyable so far," he said, having not made idle conversation for many years and wondering if it sounded as false and benign as it did to his own ears.

She dipped into a pretty curtsy, the flush of pink on her cheeks deepening. "Thank you for attending, Lord Howley." She gestured to her sisters. "These are my sisters. The Duchess of Derby, Viscountess Leigh, and the Marchioness of Chilsten."

He bowed again, ignoring the narrowed eyes and inspection each sister gave him. He wondered what they saw and what they thought of him. He had not been in society for years. Would they know anything at all?

He hoped they did not.

"You are more than welcome, Lord Howley, but how is it that we have not been introduced to you before? Have you recently returned to town?" Viscountess Leigh asked him, sidling up to Ashley and entwining her arm with her sister.

So the viscountess did not trust him. Smart woman, and he liked her all the more for it.

"I reside in London, but I do not attend the *ton's* entertainments."

"Not ever?" the Duchess of Derby queried, coming up to the other side of Ashley. Two guards he would need to get past if he wanted to speak to the one woman who had brought him here.

He bit back a grin. "Not ever, Your Grace." He did not elaborate, and Ashley stepped forward, breaking the awkward silence, and her sister's hold.

"Shall we dance, Lord Howley?"

"Ashley!" her sister, the Marchioness of Chilsten, scolded. "Maybe his lordship does not wish to dance." She met his eye, smiling a little at her sister's forwardness. "Apologies, my lord. My sister is new to society and its rules."

He reached out his hand, slipping Miss Woodville's into his. It was small and delicate and covered in silk. He wanted to strip her of the smooth confines and feel her. Revel in her touch.

He shook the thought aside. What was wrong with him, acting as if he cared? He did not. He merely was here to stop her from making a mistake. Nothing more.

"When it comes to society's rules, I too am rusty, so

long have I lived without them. But I would be honored to dance with you, Miss Woodville," he said.

She grinned, throwing a triumph glance over her shoulder to her sisters, who looked less than pleased to let her step out with him. Nevertheless, they conceded, and he escorted her onto the dance floor, other couples joining them in the Gavotte.

"So you came, my lord. I did not think I would see you here. I thought I would have to go against your orders and visit you at the hell again if I wished for another conversation."

He pulled her against him, moving them through the dance steps as the music floated through the room. "You would not dare, Miss Woodville. I forbade you to do so."

She shrugged, and his attention snapped to her delicate shoulder and the low cut of her gown. He took a calming breath, having not seen her in all her finery, the twinkling candlelight making her look ethereal and too beautiful for words.

"I thought that you would have been engaged by now. Is there no gentleman in the *ton* who has caught your heart yet?" he teased her, his words beyond what was acceptable.

Not that he cared. There was no one to listen to what he said.

Her eyes flew wide, and she glanced about, ensuring privacy. "No, my lord. There is no one, not yet at least. But the Season is young, and I have time to make a gentleman fall in love with me."

"That is true, Miss Woodville, and I'm sure they will, so long as you behave yourself and do not ruin your reputation by visiting the East End of London as you have been. I hope you have stopped your foolishness?"

"We have." She nodded. "Not since you returned us

home have we partaken in another dare. We have learned our lesson," she said, all innocence, and yet her eyes twinkled with mirth as if she were teasing him.

"Do not lie to me, Miss Woodville. It would help if you did not put your reputation at risk. No lark is worth a life lived in the shadows, where even your family and friends are frowned upon should they visit you." He knew this fact himself, so long had he lived it. Not to mention his poor mama, who had lost everything she held dear, including her husband.

Ashley studied him a moment, wondering if Lord Howley had said more than he ought just then. Had something happened in his life that had made him disappear into the shadows of the East End and never venture into the light that was Mayfair during the Season?

"You speak as if from experience, my lord." She wanted to ask him directly. Have him tell her all his secrets. He merely looked over her head as if he had not heard her.

"I see Lord Walsh and Lord Fenton seemed quite interested in your person. They have not taken their attention from you since the moment I asked you to dance."

Ashley glanced to the side of the room and spotted the earl and viscount watching her, the earl's eyes bright with interest. However, she could do without the viscount's appraisal. From the first moment she had been introduced to the viscount, she had felt as if he used Lord Walsh to work like a pack of wolves, circling his prey and then gorging on it together. She would not be dancing with Lord Fenton if she could avoid it.

"Let us hope that Lord Fenton's interest wanes in any

case, my lord," she said, not wanting to state outright that she hoped his lordship would leave her well alone.

"Fenton is an eligible gentleman. I would have thought your interest would be as great as his?" he queried.

She shook her head, frowning up at him. He stared back at her, the depth of his green eyes—like glistening emeralds that one could become lost within—captivating her. He was so handsome. His strong jaw and straight nose told of his aristocratic breeding, but that was where it ended. Lord Howley may be of noble blood, but danger and darkness floated about his very being, and she had to admit it made him all the more interesting to be around.

"Not at all. When I find the gentleman I wish to marry, he will know my interest. I do not seek Lord Fenton's attention, so I shall give him no reason to seek mine."

"You may not have a choice," his lordship said, a sardonic lift to his lips.

Ashley shrugged. "That is his issue, not mine, my lord."

"And you find Lord Walsh acceptable?" he queried, his eyes narrowed as he waited for her to reply.

"He is much more palatable than Fenton in any case. I see no reason he cannot pursue me."

"Hmm, you probably ought to reconsider that if you're looking for guidance."

She paused, studying him a moment, reveling that she was in his arms at a ball, dancing, when she had not thought to see him again. "I will ask you for guidance when and if I need it, my lord," she said, pausing. "Perhaps now you will tell me why you are in attendance? Do you, by chance, have designs on me and accepted my invitation to declare yourself?" she asked, unable to stop the grin from spreading across her lips.

His attention snapped back to her before he laughed,

his hold on her tightening. "No, I'm sorry, Miss Woodville, but my interest in you is curiosity only. That and ensuring you will not come back to visit me at the hell."

"The hell was very curious. I do wish to see more of it," she admitted, knowing that if Lord Howley had not come tonight, she would have traveled back to his gaming hell to see him again.

The thought of being alone with him made her shiver in awareness. He was so menacing and different from the other gentlemen she had met before. She wished he would attend more of these events so she could see more of him. Try to understand his lordship better.

"That I forbade," he said, the tone of his voice brooking no argument.

"You may forbid it all you like, but I'm not your wife or your sister, and I can do whatever I choose," she returned, not entirely liking that he thought he could tell her what to do.

"You do not want to be caught at my hell by me a second time. What I stated before is true. I may not be so accommodating next time."

She grinned just as the dance came to an end. "Well, my lord. Now you have made the possibility even more alluring. Whatever shall I do?" She laughed.

A muscle worked on his jaw, and for a moment, she glimpsed the hard, East End hell owner, not the gentleman earl. "You will not do that," he said, pulling her from the floor and into a darkened passage.

# CHAPTER
# SIX

Grady pulled Ashley out into the darkened corridor, closed the door behind them, and stopped. What was he doing? Was he trying to force marriage on himself by dragging her through the throng of guests and disappearing with her?

She stared up at him, a look of expectation crossing her features, and he hauled himself away from her. She was too tempting to be alone with. "You need to return to the ball this very moment. Dragging you out here was a mistake. I have nothing to say to you."

"And yet you pulled me into this part of the house anyway." She wandered about the passage, looking at several paintings on the walls. "You must have wanted to discuss something with me."

She turned and crossed her arms at her front, the action pushing her ample bosom upward and distracting his common sense. He dragged his attention back to her face and forced it to stay there.

"Word of warning before I leave. Keep away from Lord

Walsh and Fenton. They're no good and are not worth your effort. Find another to marry. Not either of them."

He started down the passage, leaving her gaping after him. He heard hurried footsteps and cringed, needing her to leave. Go now, before they were caught alone.

"Why, I can understand Fenton, but what is wrong with Lord Walsh? Why would you not recommend his lordship? Are you in possession of such high morals to even mete out such advice?" Her sarcastic tone slowed his steps.

He stopped but did not look at her. "My reputation would say otherwise, but be assured that neither of those men will give you a life worth living or a marriage of love as you wish. You will thank me for my insight one day, maybe not today, but soon enough."

Then, he left her, striding back toward the foyer and out the front door. He hailed a hackney, and when ensconced on the grimy seat, he only then sighed his relief.

His skin prickled, and his blood rushed through his veins. Grady pulled at his cravat, ripping it from his neck and opening the buttons on his shirt. Everything felt too warm, stifling, and confining.

The carriage rumbled through the streets of Mayfair, and he glanced outside, hating the life the rich and selfish lived within the Georgian mansions surrounding him. None of them had any inkling of what it was like to struggle. Of what life was like for those shunned by their gilded lives.

He did, however, and his father was the cause of that struggle. His mother deserved so much more, and when his father was dead, he would then take back everything that was his by birth and would give as much help as he could to those who kept him alive, giving him the life he now lived.

The Mayfair streets faded into the past as the seedier side of London came into view. The area was as dark and dank as it was hard and cruel. And still, it felt more like home than the opulent Mayfair location where he had left Ashley Woodville staring after him.

His hell was all that he had. It kept his mother fed and clothed and himself too and his many workers. But if that hell allowed him to help an uninformed country chit from making a grave mistake, he would venture into society and stop her from doing something she would regret forever.

The chit had already proved to be impulsive and a little naïve. He would not put it past her not to fall for pretty words and false promises and accept an offer of marriage from either Walsh or Fenton.

He ground his teeth, hating the thought of such a heinous act. She would suffer if she married either of them. He wished he could save whomever the woman was that would marry either cad, but he knew he could not scare all the women away. Some debutante would become the next countess or viscountess, and he could only hope their lives weren't as bad as he assumed they would become.

The carriage took several more minutes until it pulled up at the back of his hell. He paid the driver handsomely and went inside. Grady walked toward the front of the hell, looking in on the gaming area and noting almost a full house.

The sight made him smile, and he enjoyed seeing his guests making use of the expensive brandy and meals they offered. Not to mention several gentlemen seemed to be enjoying the company of lady guests. The night would be a profitable one.

"Out late this evening, Grady. I hope I have nothing to worry about?" Maud soothed, running her hand along his chest to his falls. He pushed her hand away, unwilling to let her grope him in front of his clientele.

"Not tonight, love. It has been a busy evening, and I'm soon to bed."

She pouted, staring up at him, and he knew if he wished, he could have her skirts lifted, even in the public locale where they now stood. He did not. The thought of fucking his mistress left a sour taste in his mouth. He wanted to sleep. Nothing more.

"I could join you. You know you will sleep better when you have me at your side."

He removed her arms from about his neck and stepped back. "I said not tonight." Grady returned upstairs and to his office. Unlocking the door, he entered and slid the bolt home, not wanting to be interrupted.

He washed his arms and face for several minutes, stripping his clothing and gaining his bed, as naked as the day he was born.

He sighed, laying back on his comfortable mattress, his arm behind his head and thoughts of a dark-haired minx tormenting him. He would dream of her tonight. He knew he would.

Damn it all to hell.

She was with him again, but this time the silk gown that adorned her sweet form was no longer. Beside his bed stood a goddess, lush breasts and slim stomach, her hips flared, giving him ample goodness to touch.

"Do you like what you see, Grady?"

He reached for her, pulling her onto his bed. She tumbled over him, her long, brown locks tickling his chest.

"I do." He rolled her beneath him, kissing her soundly. So sweet, her tongue tangling with his and leaving his cock aching for release. He kissed his way down her body, paying homage to her breasts, reveling in the feel of her undulations, her gasps of pleasure, and pleas for more.

He gave her all she wanted, making his way down her body. Her skin smelled of jasmine, so delicious his mouth watered. The tickling hairs of her mons teased his senses.

He pushed her legs aside. There was no shame or embarrassment. His dream Ashley allowed him all liberties. He needed to taste her and groaned as her sweet and musky dew settled on his lips.

"So good," he said, taking her nubbin into his mouth and suckling. She bucked beneath him, her fingers spiking into his hair. He could not get enough of her, he lathed every part of her cunny, teasing her with his tongue, but it wasn't enough.

He came up atop her, staring down at the woman who had somehow captured his sole interest—the only woman who had dragged him from this part of London to hers.

She wrapped her legs about his hips, lifting herself against him, rubbing along his manhood.

"I want you," she begged, pulling him down for a kiss.

He gave her what she wanted, drank from her mouth and rubbed her cunny with his cock.

So wet and wanton. Unable to wait a moment longer, he reached between them, guiding himself into her hot core.

She bit her lip, a sweet, needy moan slipping from her as he entered her in one long, agonizing stroke.

"Yes, Grady. Now you are mine," she sighed, her fingernails scoring his back.

And she was his. He thrust into her and took her with hard, determined strokes. Needing her to know she was his. He owned her now. She would never be with another and certainly never marry anyone else if he could help it.

He fucked her with fierce strokes. So achingly close. Her legs lifted higher, her feet crossing above his ass.

"More, Grady," she begged him, her voice husky and breathless.

He was lost now in the throes of passion. His balls tightened, and his cock stiffened further. She threw back her head and screamed his name as the first contractions of her release rippled around his cock.

It was too much. Grady came hard, pumping his pleasure into her with abandonment.

He woke with a start, his hand hard about his cock and his semen over his stomach. For a moment, he lay there, his breathing hard as he tried to recover from his dream. A dream so vivid and real that he wanted more of it.

He wanted her.

Ashley Woodville.

A woman out of his reach, except in his dreams.

# SEVEN

Even though Ashley had told Lord Howley that she and her friends would not take part in any more dares, the week since he had attended her ball had come and gone, and there were no more sightings of him.

It was Lady Anna's idea to dress up as men and travel by hackney to Lord Howley's hell. They had more than enough blunt to enjoy a night of gambling, and they had been around society long enough to know how to play cards and dice games.

Not to mention with the help of Caroline's lady's maid, their clothing, superfine coats, top hats, shirts, and embroidered waistcoats looked the epitome of a young group of lads out on their first night in London.

"You look like a man. The stubble your maid drew on your face is perfect, and looking at you, I cannot tell that you're a woman at all," Paisley said, smiling at Ashley.

It had taken them hours to get ready, and each of them had told the other's guardian or parents that they were to stay at various houses. It enabled them to remain out until the wee hours of the morning and was perfect for their next adventure.

Nerves skittered through Ashley's stomach, and she clutched her abdomen. What would Lord Howley say should he recognize them? He would be angry, that she had little doubt, but at least they chose his hell for their first night of gambling. They could have picked any other and placed themselves in far more danger than they were.

He ought to be pleased they trusted him enough with their scheme.

A wishful thought. He would scold her should he recognize any of them, especially as she promised him that she would not partake in any more dares. But what was life without some fun with friends?

"I hope we all can pull off this farce. I worry that we may run into people we may know," Paisley said, biting her lip.

"They will not recognize us. We're wearing wigs, and our breasts are wrapped and our stomachs padded. We do not look like women. Play the part of a man, and no one will look twice at you," Lady Anna stated, nodding.

The carriage pulled to a halt at the top of the lane where Lord Howley's hell was located. They jumped down, and Ashley remembered not to fiddle with her waistcoat and breeches. She was more comfortable than ever, but even so, with so little clothing, she felt naked and vulnerable.

With a stride she hoped passed as masculine, they made their way down the lane to where the door to the hell stood ajar.

Without question, they entered the building, the heavy-set, tall man at the door glancing at each of them with narrowed eyes.

Ashley wondered if he suspected them but dismissed

the notion when no one else at the hell turned even to acknowledge their arrival.

"I'm going to walk around, see what games I can join," Ashley said, moving toward the center of the room and taking note of what was being played.

She remembered to frown and appear as least feminine as she could when those who did look up took note. She spotted several gentlemen who were friends with her sisters' husbands, but none of them identified her.

She sighed in relief, hoping it would remain that way. Ashley played several rounds of whist and even partook in dice, a new game to her she had not played before.

Having won considerably more blunt than she had entered with, Ashley ordered a glass of hock, another beverage she had not tasted before, and stood near the side of the room, watching the gentlemen play.

The hairs on the back of her neck stood on end, and she glanced up to the first-floor landing, and the breath in her lungs seized.

There stood Grady Kolten, the Earl of Howley watching the room just as she was now. He leaned on the balustrade, a woman at his side with a gown that left little to anyone's imagination.

Annoyance pooled in her stomach, and she glared at the woman. Was that his lover? Did he have a mistress after all? She had not asked him such a thing, but it went without saying that he probably did. What man of his employment and status, not to mention looks, did not have a woman to warm his bed?

She sipped her beverage and swallowed hard when his eyes locked on hers. He pinned her to the spot, and she looked away, hoping he did not sense her nervousness.

Why had she looked at him at all? What if he had recognized her?

Ashley stopped herself from adjusting her short wig, the blonde hair opposite her brown and one she hoped further kept people from recognizing her.

Lord Howley stepped away from the railing and started down the stairs. Ashley held her breath when he reached the ground floor before walking in the opposite direction to where she stood.

As if a weight had been lifted from her shoulders, she leaned back against the wall to enjoy her drink and her besting of the man. How she would tease him that he had not seen her in attendance when he had warned her away.

Or perhaps not. He would be frightfully angry and taking in some of his customers, rightfully so.

She spied her friends, each of them lounging at their gaming tables, playing the perfect false gentlemen they were dressed as. Ashley debated how long they had been here and knew their time was coming to an end, that they should return home soon, lest their lie was found out. She would finish her beer and then leave.

"What the hell do you think you're doing?"

Ashley let out a high-pitched squeak that garnered a few odd looks before she schooled her features and turned to the berating Grady Kolten, who stood over her like a pillar of death.

She lifted her beer, pointing to it. "Having a drink," she managed before a look of absolute disbelief crossed his features.

"My office. Now," he warned, pushing past her and spilling a small portion of her drink over her waistcoat.

She scoffed but thought better of going against his wishes and followed him upstairs as ordered. It felt as if she were walking to her death, and she didn't doubt that maybe she was.

G rady paced his office, unable to believe he had seen Miss Woodville standing to the side of his gaming hell, hock in hand and enjoying the games afoot before her.

He recognized her immediately and hoped others had not. Even with her light-colored wig that looked as fake as the fact she was a woman pretending to be a man.

He walked to the decanter of whisky and poured himself a large dram, downing it just as the little piece of trouble walked into his office and shut the door quietly behind her.

She did not say a word. Smart, considering he wasn't sure if he wished to bellow at the stupidness of her actions.

"What are you thinking, coming back here? Especially when I told you to stay away."

She raised a defiant chin, looking down her nose at him, even though she stood a good foot shorter than he.

"We got bored and decided on more dares. Since you did not out us last time or murder us, we thought your hell as good as any to try our luck. So far, too, we have not been found out." She crossed her arms, and his attention dipped to her breasts, or lack thereof.

Had she bound them? He growled at the thought of unwrapping her like a present.

"If you think that I will allow this disregard for your safety and that of your friends, you are mistaken. I will be telling Derby of your outing, and you will be sent back to wherever you came from, and good riddance too."

She winced at his words, and he pushed aside any guilt

of speaking to her so harshly. The chit needed to learn before she ended up dead.

His words seemed to pull her from her obstinate stance, but he was mistaken if he expected her to beg him this time. Instead, she shrugged, her absurd wig not in the least disguising her high cheekbones or feminine lift to her lips.

She was pretty, even with hair as short as some chimney sweeps.

"You will do no such thing," she answered him, the sway of her hips as she came before him distracting him a moment.

"And why is that?" he asked, crossing his arms, needing to have that barrier more than ever between them. She was too disobedient for a chit of her breeding, and by God, he adored that.

"If you send me away, how will my visits amuse you?" she said, all innocence. "Admit it, until I stole into your hell, your life was as tedious as mine has been. But there is a solution, and I think you'll like it," she said, propping herself up against his desk next to him as if she owned the place.

"Really?" he drawled. "Do tell."

She grinned up at him, her sweet face making his breath catch. "My excursions about London, day and night, would be much safer if I had an escort, and I do believe I've found the perfect gentleman for my jaunts."

"Who?" he asked, knowing she better not say Lord Walsh.

Her smile never slipped. "You."

# EIGHT

"**A**bsolutely not! Are you mad?" he bellowed at her, moving to stand near the fire in his office.

Ashley shrugged, not moving from her place against his desk. "It is the perfect solution to my issue. I want to see more of London, not just the glittery, pretty part that I've been privy to so far. And, well, you live in the less-favorable locale but know the limits of keeping safe that I do not. With your help and company, I shall stop all dares and merely ask you to escort me about instead."

He stared at her as if she were some kind of simpleton. "Where do you wish to go?" he asked, running a hand through his hair. The action left him looking bedraggled, and heat kissed her cheeks. She pushed away from the desk, going to his decanter of whiskey and pouring herself a glass, her mouth parched.

She sipped, coughed, and then sipped again. "I wish to go everywhere you're willing to take me. I would love to see the inside of Whites if you're a member. As you know, women are not allowed. An absurd rule that ought to be outlawed."

His lips twitched, but he did not say a word, merely narrowed his eyes. Did that mean he was at least thinking about what she asked of him? She hoped it was so.

"I would like to see how the other half of London survives. Even if that life is not as pretty and safe as my own. I want to see the world for what it is, not just the glittering ballrooms." She came over to him, meeting his eye. "I'm an heiress, you know, and when I marry, so long as I marry a man who loves me, I shall be able to do whatever I want."

His eyes widened before he asked, "And what do you want to do? Do not all gently bred young ladies wish to play pianoforte and embroider cushions, ride horses, and attend tea parties?"

Ashley rolled her eyes. The man was clearly misinformed. No woman could only want to do such menial tasks as the ones he listed. Such a life would never do at all. "I want to help those less fortunate than myself. I want to help the motherless children of London. Give them a better future than they started with. Find them employment when they're old enough and with some education and ensure that until they're capable, they have housing and clothing to give them the best start they could possibly have.

"I want to be informed and know what people mean when they talk about things. As for that matter, I want to talk about everything. No one talks about anything important. It was one of the reasons my friends and I started our little game. It was much more fun than going from ball to ball that was oftentimes more boring than being at home before the fire."

"Honorable idea indeed, but unlikely to occur if you marry Lord Walsh."

She waved his words aside. "I do not want to talk about Lord Walsh or any of the young men courting me this Season. I want to know if you'll accompany me to wherever I want, and that includes workhouses and Whites, Vauxhall whenever I wish, and not grumble about it when you do. And if you help me, Lord Howley, I shall not visit you here again. I promise," she said, crossing her chest with her hand.

"I think it would be easier for me to tell Derby and be done with you."

"Do you really wish to be done with me?" she asked, giving him her best coquettish look, hoping that was not the case.

His eyes sparkled with something she did not understand before he blinked, and it was gone. He sighed, glancing at the ceiling, as if wishing for divine intervention.

He would not receive any from above.

"Very well, I shall take you to the places you wish to visit, but you will need to be dressed as a man to enable such an act. Can you change into that outfit," he said, gesturing to her person, "and sneak out of the ducal residence without being caught?"

"I think so, but an even better idea would be that I change here. I would have to visit you then again, but I can put the wig on in the carriage before I arrive so no one would become wise of my identity."

"So you are already going back on your word not to visit here again."

She gave him the sweetest smile she could summon, which by his less-than-pleased visage did not seem to work as she wanted it to. "Not really. I would not go through the front door like this evening. I would sneak in through the back."

His lordship shook his head, disbelief crossing his features. "So the only way to keep you safe is to do as you want. What do I get out of it should I help you, Miss Woodville?" he asked.

Ashley downed her whisky and handed him her glass. "The pleasure of my company, my lord," she said, walking from the room, unable to stop the grin on her lips.

He wasn't a mean man. He would help her, and what fun there was to be had. Now she merely needed to decide where to go and when.

T he following days Ashley spent at home sorting through Derby's clothing that sat in trunks collecting dust in the attic. Superfine coats and marvelous embroidered waistcoats that he had commissioned when he was a younger man seemed the perfect fit for a woman of her size.

She had several outfits, all folded and sorted at the bottom of her traveling trunk that sat packed away in her dressing room.

Ashley attended several balls and one dinner at Lady Shaw's as expected the following few nights, and although the evenings were enjoyable, her mind would not stop thinking about her first outing with the Earl of Howley.

Grady Kolten.

Would he allow her to call him by his given name if they were to be friends? Or perhaps he would prefer to be called Howley instead.

She sat in the drawing room, her sister Hailey knitting white booties for her forthcoming child. The duchess had announced she would have a child before the end of the year.

Ashley was happy for her. Hailey all but glowed as she

knitted away, most likely lost in thoughts of what a happy family they would have before Christmas.

"I think I shall stay in this evening if you do not mind, sister. We've been so busy attending London events that I feel I need a day or two at home. Would you be disappointed to attend this evening's ball without me?" Ashley asked, preferring not to pretend to have a headache or sore throat to get out of the night's entertainment. She did not want anyone hovering over her or staying behind to keep her company as she pretended to get better.

Hailey placed her knitting in her lap with a concerned frown. "Is there something the matter, dearest? Are you unwell? Do you wish for me to call the doctor to examine you?"

Ashley waved her concern aside, sitting forward to pour herself a fresh cup of tea. "Not at all. Nothing is wrong. I'm merely weary and wish for an early night," she fibbed and pushed down the guilt that she was lying to a beloved sister.

"We can cancel this evening. I know Derby would not mind. He's not one for balls and parties much these days," Hailey said, rubbing her small stomach.

Ashley smiled, sipping the hot tea. "I know he is not, but I'm not unwell. I just do not wish to go. I need a day or two at home, that is all. There is no need for anyone to watch me. I'll be perfectly fine here with the servants. And in any case, I will be abed early. I feel I need it," she said, smiling at her sister, who continued to study her as if trying to fathom if she were in earnest or not.

"Well...if you're sure. The ball is only around the corner from this house, walking distance, as you know. We shall not be far away if you need us to return home."

"I know, and I thank you," she said.

"Lord Walsh will be disappointed you will not be in attendance. He seems eager to court you." Hailey glanced up, meeting her eye. "Does your interest point in the same direction as Lord Walsh?"

Ashley thought about his lordship, handsome but too influenced by Lord Fenton for her liking. The man needed to form some of his own opinions to be of any interest.

Not to mention the thought of any of the men previously courting her seemed to pale into insignificance now that she knew Lord Howley. How would she ever stop thinking of the man so she could form an opinion on others who did seek a wife as much as she sought a husband?

She was sure Lord Howley, a hell owner with a mistress, did not want a wife or a future with children. He seemed more than pleased to remain the bachelor he was. A wife would only be a complication he did not seek.

She needed to remember that whenever her heart lurched at the sight of him. He was not for her. In all truth, he was an outcast to society, a man no longer part of the *ton* unless one attended his gaming hell in East London.

He was not for her, and even if she did secretly wish that were not so, he would not change for her, and she did not expect him to.

# NINE

G rady paced the corridor outside his office, the visions haunting his mind of what was happening in his room right at this moment, making keeping still impossible.

Ashley Woodville would be the death of him. If not by his want of the meddling minx, then by her family, who would want his head on a spike after they found out what he was up to with her.

"And you're sure we're not going to be in a hired box with the other toffs? I want to be in the pit of the theater. It looks like a much more amusing place to be when I was there last," she called out from his room, her voice muffled through the door.

"Oh really. And why is that?" Not that he, in truth, wanted to know her reasoning.

"All the dandies seem to accumulate there, and those who stand in the pit seem to laugh and enjoy the night much more than I ever have," she stated.

All true. The pit was a place for entertainment, meeting friends, and heckling the actors on stage.

"I do have a box, Miss Woodville, but if you wish to sit high in the stalls, you'll have to attend with one of your friends or Derby. I do not use it." And nor would he tell her as to the reason why.

"Not at all, my lord." She went quiet a moment—more shuffling. "Almost done," she called out from inside the room.

He shook his head, running his hands through his hair. He walked to the end of the hall and glanced out the small window that overlooked the back entrance to the hell. A few of his men unloaded a cart with fresh produce, taking it into the kitchens located in the venue's basement.

He walked back to the door, knocking. "Come now. We will be late if you do not hurry," he called, fighting the urge to peek through the keyhole like some desperate fiend. Would he see her binding her breasts? How she had made her ample bosom disappear was a mystery he would love to solve.

"You may come in. I'm just tying up my boot laces," she explained.

Grady opened the door and was seized with want for the chit. She was dressed as a man, her clothes finer than his. And rightfully so since she had stolen them from her ducal brother-in-law. But her hair was down, her long, curling locks covering her shoulders. He devoured the sight of her. Lovely, slim legs and delectable ass that fit her breeches perfectly. He knew there were generous breasts beneath her shirt. Bundled flat. The knowledge and thought of unwrapping her made looking at her painful.

"Put your wig on and let us go. You will miss the opening scene if we do not leave now," he barked, his tone one formed from frustration.

She quickly plaited her hair and slipped it under a short, blonde wig she produced from a nearby valise. She twirled before him, clearly pleased with her transformation. "What do you think? Will I pass as a man, do you believe?" she asked, smiling.

Grady groaned. "If you twirl like that again, you will fool no one with your pretense." He started out of the room and down the passage, not bothering to wait for her.

She hurried after him, catching him just as they made the back door. "Thank you for doing this, my lord. I truly appreciate it."

He strode to his carriage, climbing up, not bothering to help her precede him.

She stared, wide-eyed as he settled on the squabs. "Get in, Ashley. You're a man, remember? Do not expect me to help you into the carriage or for you to jump in first. You'll give yourself away to my staff before we even make it to the theater."

His words seemed to pull her from her stupefied trance, and she tumbled into the carriage as it lurched forward before she had made her seat. Her ass landed on his lap, her delectable curves teasing him, and he clasped her waist, taking a moment to enjoy her in his arms before he set her on the seat across from him.

"Try to not be seen on my lap either, Ashley. I'm not known as a man who prefers my own sex."

Her eyes widened, and she stared at him, clearly contemplating the thought. "Are there such occurrences?" she asked him.

He closed his eyes, praying for patience. "Yes, for both sexes, and that is all I'm going to tell your delicate, sheltered ears about it."

She pouted at him, and he frowned. "And do not look like that either. You're acting too feminine. You will be caught, and then I'll be called out on a field of honor. And if you do not mind, I do not want to die merely because you manipulated me into helping you complete this foolhardy dream of yours to see the 'Real London'."

"Fine," she said, her lips thinning into a displeased line. "I shall do better even when we're not in public." She glanced out the window a moment. "What will you call me? I should probably have a name since people may ask you."

All true, and something he had been debating the last couple of nights they had not seen each other. "I think Ash for your first name will do well, and you are more likely to come to that instead of calling you by some different random name. But as for your last, I think you will take my mother's maiden name of Renolds."

"So I'll be your cousin then, visiting London, we should say," she suggested. "What fun we'll have. A lovely family reunion."

"Except we're not related," he drawled. Was she always so happy and excited by everything? He was not so certain being around all this sunshine would be good for him. He preferred the dark shadows of London, not the warmth and light that Miss Woodville brought with her.

A shley strode up the steps of the Theatre Royal alongside Lord Howley. "So I suppose I should call you Howley since we're cousins. Or you could give me leave to call you Grady?" she suggested, grinning across from him and gaining a glare in return.

The man was so grumpy but quite sweet, no matter

how distempered he was about helping her see the London that people of her ilk rarely viewed.

This was good for her, and it would give her an appreciation for what she had while also knowing what she needed to do to help others. Not to mention, she would get to see the inside of Whites and best the gentlemen of the *ton* who thought themselves so high and mighty to keep the women out.

"You will not call me Grady," he bit back, a muscle in his jaw working. "You can, however, call me Howley. That will be appropriate."

Satisfied, Ashley nodded to those who spoke to Howley as they entered the large foyer of the theater. There were men bustling into the building, those with status and fortune started up the stairs to their boxes while others, people like herself, remained on the ground floor and headed into the pit.

"What is the play that we're to see this evening?" she asked, keeping her voice low and as masculine as she thought possible.

Lord Howley shrugged. "I have no idea. I'm sure it is nothing spectacular. Do not get your hopes up," he drawled, leading the way.

She followed, but the crowd, jostling and rushing to enter, separated them. He stopped, sensing her lagging, and waited for her to catch up. The moment she did, his hand fluttered against the lower part of her back before he thought better of his measure and snatched his hand away.

Ashley made a point of looking at the table of events, ignoring what his touch had made her feel. What was it about the man at her side that drew her to him? He was not the warmest soul, and he had long lived outside the bounds of polite society, so as to be almost feral.

Ashley glanced at him, his handsome profile making her want to sigh in approval. Even knowing all that she did about him, he was here with her, giving her what she wanted. He did not have to be so accommodating. He could have told her to bugger off. He could have told the duke of her escapades, and at this very moment, she could be in a carriage on the way home to Grafton.

But she was not. She was here. With him. And never in her life had an evening at the theater been such a marvelous adventure.

They made their way to the front of the pit and waited with other patrons. Ashley looked up toward the first floor, where the *ton* sat. The sight of her brother-in-law, the duke, and her sister made her blood run cold.

Would they recognize her? She adjusted her wig, forcing herself not to look again lest they notice her interest.

"Keep your eyes on the stage, and no one behind us or upstairs is likely to realize who you are. You're merely another head in the sea of the less-cultured. The *demimonde* often stand here or gentlemen of the *ton* and their mistresses."

"Do you often use the pits to watch plays, or do you really attend using a box upstairs, like all the other entitled people in London and just told me otherwise?" she asked him. "You're an earl and future duke after all. No one could fault you if you did."

He cleared his throat, not bothering to meet her eye. "I do not use anything of my father's. He's still alive, as you well know, and until he dies, nothing of his is mine."

Not for the first time, Ashley wondered what happened between them. What was it that occurred that had enabled an earl to live in the East End, run a gaming hell, and keep from society? And why would a father, a duke, allow such isolation?

She pondered that just as the curtains opened, the first actor appeared on the stage, bellowing their first lines, and Ashley forgot all about her musings and simply lost herself in the crowd, engrossed in the play like everyone else.

For now, at least.

# CHAPTER
# TEN

G rady kept his attention on the play, no small feat when the distracting Ashley Woodville stood beside him, all smiles and laughter. It had been a mistake in bringing her here. Even though it was a requirement of hers, she was too lively, pretty, and smiley to be a man of serious countenance. Few would believe that the bubbly lad beside him was his cousin.

Already a few had thrown him curious looks, and he had been forced to stare the bastards down.

"Remember to look less feminine," he reminded her for the hundredth time.

She rolled her eyes and continued to smile and laugh as the play continued.

This would never do. How was he to keep her under control if this is how she was the very first evening he had obliged her curiosity.

Not that he could hate her for wanting to see the London he knew and few others ever viewed. It was noble of her to want to help, to learn and know the secrets kept from women such as herself, but he doubted she could do

54

much. Certainly, if she married Lord Walsh, he would get his hands on her fortune and do whatever he wished with the funds. His wife would have little say in the matter.

Grady relaxed his hands and pushed all thoughts of the bastard Walsh from his mind. He was here with Ashley, no lord would be courting her this evening, and after the play was finished, he would ensure she returned home safe and sound, and he would be done with her. For this evening in any case.

He covertly watched her enjoy the play, her smile and bright eyes telling him without words how much she relished it. He had seen it before, and from the pit where they now stood. Except for that night, he had been with his mistress, not a debutante new to the marriage mart and looking for a husband.

Dear Lord, what had he gotten himself into with her?

Two hours later the play ended and she sighed, slumping against her chair and looking up at him with such pleasure he forgot that she was playing a man.

"That was wonderful," she said, her voice feminine and wistful.

"Remember where you are, Ash," he stated. The crowd was departing, and Grady glanced up to his box, expecting it to be empty. It was not. His father sat in the only chair in the viewing room, staring at him. The duke's eyes narrowed, and the distaste on his visage was almost palatable, even this far away.

Ashley came to stand at his side, following his line of sight. "Is that your father?" she asked. "You look similar," she stated, moving past him as if to leave.

Grady pulled himself together and followed her, ignoring his father, whom he had not seen in several years. It was odd he was at the play at all. He was not a man who enjoyed such frivolities. Perhaps he had heard of him attending Whites last week and wanted to ensure that Grady did not think to step back into society anytime soon.

He came out into the foyer and started outside, looking to hire a hackney.

"I did not think they allowed curs like you to attend plays. You ought to know your place, boy, and remain in the East End where you belong."

Grady sighed and prayed for patience before he turned and faced his sire.

"I have nothing to say to you. Leave," he said, hating that the man thought it his place to say anything to him at all. He had lost all right to speak to him the moment he disowned his mother and, in time, himself due to a situation not of her doing.

"I tolerate your gaming hell, but I do not want to hear of you attending any balls or Whites again. Do I make myself clear? While I cannot disinherit you, by God, I will not stand for you to blacken the Blackhaven name while breath still enters my body."

A hackney cab rolled to a stop before them, and he could feel Ashley's riveted attention on them both. He did not want her to know of his father and the shame his actions had caused Grady and his mother.

"I have never blackened the name. You do that well enough yourself," he returned, climbing up onto the squabs and slamming the door closed in the duke's face once Ashley had hastily followed him.

The carriage lurched forward, and he took a calming breath, ignoring Ashley's wide eyes that unnervingly stared at him.

"Was that your father the duke or not? He seems angry

at you," she said, her voice light and airy, Ashley no longer pretending to be a man.

"That's because he is," he said. "I did not think he would be at the theater this evening, but I know why he was. We should not cross his path again. Not when you're looking to visit places that the *beau monde* are loath to admit exist."

Her mouth thinned into a displeased line, and he did not like that she looked at him with pity. He did not want anyone to pity him. He was wealthy and legitimate, no matter what his father thought, and one day he would be the duke. And nothing that his father said or did could change that fact.

"That is very sad. Your father should not have spoken so terribly to you." She reached out, taking his hand. Grady reveled in her comforting hold before common sense returned, and he pulled away. Moving to sit as far away from her as possible.

"I'm sorry," she said.

He could hear the sincerity in her tone. There was so much she did not know and never would if he could help it. And he did not need her sympathy, his life was full, and nothing, not even his father the duke, could touch him now. Or hurt him ever again.

The following evening Ashley attended Lord Flower's ball. She had danced with several gentlemen, but the night, as entertaining and pleasant to catch up with friends as it had been, was missing a little charm with the absence of Lord Howley.

She had thought he might attend another ball since he made an appearance at her coming out, but it did not seem it was so. Where was he? Was he at his club or enjoying other, more private, entertainments with his lady friends?

The thought soured the syllabub in her mouth, and she put down her spoon, determined to stop torturing herself with thoughts of a man who in no way would be thinking of her.

Unless he was thinking of ways to get rid of her and stop their outings. An outing that, unfortunately, would not be happening this evening due to her commitment to the ball her sister demanded she attend.

Tomorrow evening, however, she wanted to do as she wished. There was to be an outdoor ball at Vauxhall. Of course, the *beau monde* were not to attend, only the *demi-mondaine* of society was invited, but she was desperate to go.

Not only to see how the other half of society lived but to be alone with Grady. Of course, he had not given her leave to use his name, but she wanted to see his reaction when she called him by his given name.

Would his eyes darken in awareness, a mirror image of hers? Ashley picked up her spoon, stirring the syllabub to a sloppy mess as she listened to Lord Walsh speak to Derby over a horse coming up for auction at Tattersalls.

She took a fortifying breath to get herself through the remainder of the night. There were not so many hours left, and her dance card was full. She would not be too bored.

Even so, watching Lord Walsh talk, little nuances that she had not picked up before became more noticeable. He was not as handsome as Grady. That was a given. And she did not think he was kind. Certainly, his friend Lord Fenton was rumored to be a highly disgraceful cad.

Lord Walsh would do well to gain better friends, but should she marry him, her social sphere would be the same as his, and Ashley wasn't so certain she wanted to be around Lord Fenton any more than she had to be.

She did not like or trust the man, and she certainly did not think he would be a good influence on Lord Walsh.

Lady Hirch sauntered past their table, and Ashley watched under hooded lashes as Lord Walsh's attention snapped to the lady and watched her, his appreciation for her low-bodice gown not missed by Ashley.

She glanced at her sister across from her. Hailey raised one brow, having seen his lordship's interest as she had, the duchess's disappointment clear to read on her features.

No, he would not be faithful, and she wanted a husband who would not warm another bed in all the world unless it was hers. She could not stomach sharing the man she loved, not that she loved Lord Walsh, but that wasn't to say that she may not have fallen in love with him in time.

Grady's warning about the man floated through her mind, and she was thankful for it. He may not circulate in this society, but he knew its workings, and something told Ashley he was right in his estimations on Lord Fenton and Walsh.

They were two gentlemen who fed the other's bad habits, and she wanted none of it, even if so many other ladies did.

CHAPTER

# ELEVEN

Ashley managed to return home early from the Mason's rout the following evening. Her sister Hailey had repeatedly asked if she was enjoying the Season and why she wished to return home so soon, especially after several gentlemen had whisked her out to dance one after another upon her arrival.

But the rout was not where she wanted to be. All day nerves had skittered through her belly each time she thought of Grady. Would he meet her at the gates of the Vauxhall Pleasure Gardens as agreed?

Ashley checked her wig was in place and pulled the small black cap she wore this evening to a tilt, making her look like a street urchin she had often seen running about on her way out to Lord Howley's hell.

This evening she had placed a little bit of coal ash on her cheeks and neck, making her look less clean than normal. With her skin that looked as smooth as milk, she had wanted to do something to make her appear more like everyone else who was not part of Mayfair.

The carriage rolled to a halt before Vauxhall's entrance,

and she sat there for several minutes, looking to see if Lord Howley was present. She could not see him, and disappointment stabbed at her that he had not come.

Was he not going to attend? Had something happened to him? She swallowed the dread that thought conjured and instead put his absence down to him not wanting to join her.

Others, however, were more than happy to attend the evening. Revelers streamed into the gardens, and from her carriage, she could hear the minstrels playing music for those who wished to dance.

Well, she would not allow a man's absence to stop her from doing what she wished. She jumped out of the carriage, paid the driver, and followed everyone else into the gardens.

No one paid her mind, even if she were shorter than most men present. Several ladies of ill repute grinned and fluttered their eyelashes at her, and Ashley tipped her head, more than happy to play the part of rogue for the evening.

It did not take long before the orchestra at a circular grand rotunda and the many dancers before them came into view. Ashley stood at the side of the makeshift outdoor ballroom, not quite believing what she was seeing.

Men and women drank and laughed, talked and flirted, but the ladies and their absence of modesty were for all to see and ogle, as most men were doing.

She did not see anyone she knew and was thankful for it, but the men were boisterous, and of a different ilk than she was used to. A thread of unease pooled low in her belly that maybe this was a mistake. A night of revelry at Vauxhall was all well and good, but perhaps this time, she had bitten off more than she could handle.

Being here alone was dangerous. Should she be fleeced

of her money, she would have no way of returning home, not unless she walked. What would she do then?

"Come, my lord, dance with me?" a feminine voice slurred beside Ashley, and without the chance to answer, she was dragged out into the fray. The orchestra started playing a country dance, and trying to forget her concerns, Ashley threw herself into the jig, trying to remember to play the man she was portraying.

"You're a pretty boy, that's for certain. Looking for a little lady attention this evening, are yer?" she asked Ashley, smiling and showing stained, yellow teeth.

Ashley could not help but feel for the woman and the hard life she undoubtedly lived. Happy or not, being a whore was certainly not what the woman had always wanted for her life. Not originally, in any case. These were the women she wished to help, to give a choice to, no matter what that choice was. To make their lives safer.

"Not tonight, I'm afraid. But I'm more than happy to dance with you," Ashley answered, hoping that would be good enough for the woman whose size was double what Ashley's was.

The lady stopped dancing in the middle of the outdoor ballroom and placed her hands on her wide hips. "What ye doing here then? If ye don't want me to tickle ye pickle, why dance at all?"

Ashley shrugged, unsure how to answer without giving offense. "Because I wanted to dance with beautiful women without anything else."

Her words brought a flush to the lady's face before she threw back her head and laughed, holding her large stomach for good measure. "Oh, you're a funny one, are ye not? Beautiful woman? Are ye blind as well as frigid, lad?" she asked Ashley.

"I'm neither," Ashley answered, ignoring that several men and women were watching keenly from the side.

"I expect to be paid, even for a dance, but I'm more than happy to have ye bend me over for an extra shilling."

"Bend her over!" shouted a man from the side, holding his manhood in his breeches and moving in a way that said without words what he imagined Ashley doing to the whore.

"That will not be necessary," Ashley reached into her pocket for her money and felt...nothing. She frowned, patted her waist, and still, the little amount of coin she had brought with her was no longer there.

Had she placed it in her coat pocket? She checked there as well and scanned the ground. Maybe she had dropped it while dancing, but still, she could not see her pin money.

"Ye do not have my coin, do ye?" the woman accused, her lip turning up in distaste. "Oh well, my man will not be happy with you."

A mocking laugh came from somewhere behind Ashley before she was pushed in the back, making her stumble. "So you dinna have the blunt to pay for Maggie's time she spent with you? Then yes, I do think we have an issue," he drawled.

Panic assailed her, and without another thought, Ashley ran. With the noise of the ball, the laughter, and the music, she could not hear if anyone chased her, but fear clawed up her spine as to what they would do to her should they catch her. She pushed her legs to move faster, trying to swerve and duck through the multitude of guests to get away.

And then she felt it. The touch of a hand on her back, before that hand clasped a handful of her coat and pulled her to a stop.

She flailed and tried to drop out of her jacket. The man at her back pushed her onto the ground, and she hit the lawned surface with an *ummph*, her chin hitting the soil.

"I want the money. Now, lad, before I beat it out of ye."

Ashley rolled onto her back, trying to scoot backward from the heavy-set man who looked three times her size. What was she going to do? Would he really strike her?

The anger resonating from his snarling face told her he would, and she would be powerless to stop it. She cringed. Why had she come here without Grady? Whatever made her believe she was capable of looking after herself in situations like this when it was clear that she was not?

"I'm sorry. I do not have any money. It must have been stolen or lost, but I only danced with your lady. I did not use her services," she said, hoping to clarify any confusion if the man before her had any.

"The dance requires payment, and if ye cannot pay, then you will pay in other ways. Do I make myself clear?" the man threatened, leaning over her and pointing his grimy finger in her face.

Oh dear God, she was going to die.

"Stand back. Now," a familiar voice growled at Ashley's side, and she looked up to see Grady standing over the man who was threatening her. She sucked in a startled gasp at the murderous rage that mottled his normally handsome visage.

He was angry. She could see it as clear as day, not to mention his tone was one of deadly intent that even she would not refuse to obey.

The man stood, pulling down his jacket and puffing up his chest in an effort to make himself stand as tall as Grady. It did little to help.

"He owes money for a dance with my girl. He either pays for it, or I'll make him pay for it."

"You will do no such thing," Grady drawled, having not yet looked at her. "How much did the dance cost?" he asked, seemingly bored by the situation now.

"Two shillings and all will be well."

Grady flipped him the small copper coins and then stepped toward the man, all but nose to nose. "You will never threaten my friend again. Do I make myself clear? Had you touched him, you would not have liked the repercussions. Be wary of who you threaten. Do you understand?"

The man narrowed his eyes and looked as if he would disobey Grady's command, but something in Grady's face stopped him from making that mistake, and he nodded, conceding the point. "Understood. 'Ave a good night," he said before disappearing into the crowd.

Ashley looked up at Grady, her seat on the grassy lawn seemingly a safer place than before the man who glared down at her with just as much threatening presence as the one before.

"What the hell do you think you are doing?" he bellowed, reaching down and yanking her to stand.

Before she could reply, he hauled her toward the path that led out of the gardens and away from the festivities. Ashley did not say a word, there was plenty of time to explain, and right now, all she wanted to do was return home. She had enough of her night of enlightenment and study of how the other side of the *ton* lives. It was found wanting, and not without a good dose of anxiety that she doubted she would ever forget.

CHAPTER

# TWELVE

Grady held on to his temper for as long as he could, but the moment he saw his carriage—a haven where he could place Ashley and keep her safe for the time he had her with him—his blood boiled a second time.

The sight of Ashley lying on the cold ground, threatened by a man, and not just any man, but one who could have killed her, placed his heart in his mouth. She could have been beaten to death, and the man would not have known she was female, not that he would have cared in truth. But Ashley was unable to withstand any kind of physical assault.

Had he not arrived, had he not seen the commotion and investigated it, he might have missed her.

He clasped under her arm and tossed her into his carriage before following her inside. He banged on the roof, and the carriage lurched forward, away from Vauxhall and the danger that lurked in the gardens when such events as the one taking place right at this minute were underway.

"Thank you for helping me. I owe you a great debt," she

whispered, her voice without its usual opinionated and self-assured tone.

Grady took a calming breath, but it did little to cool his ire. "What on earth were you thinking, woman! You could have been killed, beaten to an inch of your life. How would you explain your bloodied, broken body to your guardian, the duke? Your actions this evening not only place yourself in danger but your family. Had your actions become known, not just yourself would have been ruined."

He expected an apology, but instead, she raised her defiant chin and glared back at him. "And who's fault would that have partly been? Yours, I should imagine, as you were supposed to meet me at Vauxhall. Where were you? Too busy with a lady friend of your own to remember me waiting for you here?"

"Even if I had a lady friend, that is none of your business. I was running late. You ought to have enough sensible thought to remain in the carriage as instructed until I arrived. You ought to have known I would have come for you, even if late."

His words seemed to douse a little of her temper, but the mulish turn of her lips told him she was still mad.

Well, damn it, so was he.

"You did not want to help me in the first place. I did not think you would arrive when you were not here at the allotted time. I apologize for going in without you, but it was not my fault what happened while there."

"And what did happen?" he asked, settling back in the squabs and crossing his arms, anything to stop himself from reaching for her and wrenching her into his hold where he knew she was safe. Protected and warm from the cold, outside world that wanted to do her harm.

"The woman forced me to dance with her, and although

that was entertaining, they then started to demand payment when I would not go off with her to do other things."

Grady swallowed, knowing what type of other things they wanted her to do. Dear heavens, what was he doing to allow the woman before him to go out and experience such lifestyles far beneath her own. He ought to be horse-whipped for allowing her to persuade him. Not that she had convinced him, she had told him she would do it with or without his help, and he could not allow that. Had he not known of her plans, this evening was an example of why he could not let her out of his sight on such adventures. She would end up getting herself killed.

"Why did you not pay for the dance and be done with it?"

Ashley rolled her eyes, and the sight made him want her even more. "I tried, but when I reached into my pocket, the money I had placed there was gone."

"So the whore fleeced you before demanding more from you. You ought to have said back at Vauxhall. I would have beaten the bastard demanding payment for trying such antics."

"I think someone did steal from me, but I'm not certain it was the woman who did that to me. It could have been anyone. I may have even lost it while dancing."

"Unlikely." Grady studied her. Her clothing was covered in grass and dirt from the lawn, but why was it down her front? He leaned forward, clasped her jaw, and tilted her head toward him. "What has happened to your chin? It's bleeding?" His stomach twisted into knots at the sight of the small cut and the scuffing of dirt throughout the wound. He reached into his pocket and pulled out his hand-kerchief, dabbing at the cut as carefully as he could while trying to clean it of grime. "Did the bastard hit you?" The fury that thrummed through him caught him unaware, and he forced himself to calm down. To relax and not frighten her more than she already was after this night.

She stared at him, her large, brown eyes capturing his awareness. The pit of his stomach lurched hot with desire for the woman before him. Never had he ever reacted to a woman with such need and the overwhelming desire to keep her safe, happy...

His.

"I was running from him. Trying to get away. He pushed me from behind, and I tripped and fell. It is nothing." She attempted to push his hands away, but he refused to relent his hold.

"Let me clean it. You will not want it to get infected," he said, knowing too well that he did not want to see her wound infected, and Ashley laid low with a fever and illness.

His being late was the reason she was alone. He could not bear the guilt such actions had brought upon her.

She allowed him his way, and he cleaned the wound as carefully as he could. Blood oozed onto his handkerchief, a good sign that it was at least ridding itself of any dirt and grime, more than it was before.

Ashley sucked in a breath. Grady looked up to see a tear slip down her cheek, that too smudged with some sort of grime.

"I'm sorry you're hurt," he whispered, kissing the lone tear away. The moment his lips touched her soft, warm cheek, he knew it for the mistake it was.

He felt her tense, and she ought to be nervous. He was as bad if not worse than many of the men who attended Vauxhall this evening who frightened her. Grady shut his eyes, forcing himself to retreat, to forget what he had just done.

But of course, Miss Woodville was having none of it. Her hands reached out, clasping the lapels of his coat, holding him near. They were so close, but an inch separating them, and his body hardened with that truth.

She was so unlike anyone he had ever known. She stared at him, her eyes unable to hide the longing and need she felt for him. She was such an oddity, dressed in men's clothing, a short, blonde wig atop her head, and even with all her attempts at looking masculine, he knew better.

There was not an ounce of masculinity to her at all. She was all womanly curves, pretty eyes, and kissable lips that he wanted to claim.

He wanted her and no one else.

"You kissed me," she finally said. "You kissed my cheek."

He swallowed, wondering if his kiss had muddled her mind a little, or as much as his own. He fought to control the need spiraling out of control within him, but it was no use. He could not stop now that he'd touched her. And damn him all the way to hell or the East End, he needed to, at least once in his life, act the gentleman and move away from her.

"An attempt to console you, that is—"

Her lips smashed against his, halting his words of denial. She did not move, merely held herself against him, and he fought not to react. To give her what she wanted.

But the moment he felt her pull away, his desire overtook all common sense, and he gave her what she wanted. What he wanted. He dropped the handkerchief to the floor, clasped her face, and took control of the kiss.

And what a kiss it was.

Her shocked gasp gave him leave to invade her mouth.

His tongue tangled with hers. The kiss, her first, he was sure, was not soft or slow, but hard and fast. He devoured her mouth, taking his fill, giving her no leave to pull away or slow his onslaught.

From the moment she entered his hell, he knew one day he would have her like this.

He wrenched the wig from her head, her long, brown locks spilling over her shoulders. Grady pulled back, looking at her with renewed awe. She was magnificent, a diamond of the first water, and alone with him.

He ought to be ashamed for the thoughts that tormented his mind, but the way Ashley looked at him right at this moment, he couldn't help but think that she, too, was thinking the same thing as he.

And that thought meant one thing.

He was doomed.

CHAPTER

# THIRTEEN

Ashley forgot all about the cut on her chin or her disastrous night at Vauxhall the moment Grady kissed her cheek. An intoxicating urgency for the man thrummed through her and would not relent.

She knew to her very core that she could not let him go, to allow him to pull away. What if she never saw him again? What if he refused to help her gain a little insight into how others less fortunate than she lived?

Not that she wanted to repeat her error of Vauxhall, but she did want to help people, and she needed to know the ins and outs of London outside of Mayfair to do that well.

But none of that mattered now. Not when Grady Kolten kissed her and left her floundering on a sea of need.

And then she had boldly kissed him back. Maybe even the whore at Vauxhall would have been impressed. She had reached for him and stolen what she had longed for since the moment she had seen him.

One that left her reeling for purchase.

But the one kiss was not enough. She wanted far more

from him, and she would get what she wanted no matter the cost.

Ashley pushed Grady back against the squabs and settled onto his lap. She could feel all of him with breeches on and not a shift and several layers of a silk gown separating them. The muscles of his legs tightened as he adjusted to her being in his lap.

Her hand settled against his chest as her other slipped about his neck. Would he move her away, place her back on the seat across from him? Without giving him a moment to think clearly, she kissed him a second time and moaned at the deliciousness of it.

His mouth welcomed her. His tongue tangling with hers made her toes curl in her leather boots. Oh dear lord, this was heaven. He was a rogue sent down to torment her with wickedness.

She moaned as his hand squeezed her waist, the top of his thumb grazing the underside of her breast. Would he touch her there? Her nipples pebbled to hardened peaks at the thought, and never in her life had she wanted to reach down more and force him to touch her.

"I should not be doing this with you. It's wrong," he whispered between kisses that left her wits spiraling.

"How can something that feels so wonderful be wrong?" she answered, kissing him anew.

He hoisted her higher on his lap, and the hardness that pushed against her outer thigh told her all she needed to know. He found this interlude as arousing as she did. This heat, the unrelenting ache that tormented her between her thighs, had to be what so many women talked of with their lovers.

Was this why her sisters were so content and happy in

their marriages? If so, she could understand why they spent so much time locked away in their suite of rooms.

"If you had any idea of what I want to do to you, Ashley, you would not be so bold."

His gravelly tone made her shiver with need. "Tell me what you want to do to me. I want to know," she said, taking the opportunity to kiss her way up his neck. The scent of sandalwood and spice wafted from his skin. Had he bathed today? The thought of him lathing his skin, soaking naked in a tub of water, made her squirm.

He growled, his hand clasping the inside of her thigh to rub her leg against his engorged manhood.

She kissed beneath his ear, being so bold as to run her tongue along his skin. He turned his head, taking her mouth in a punishing kiss. Ashley threw herself into his onslaught, not scared by the reaction she had to his every touch, his every word, but entranced, enthralled, and utterly his to do with as he pleased, whatever that may be.

"You do not want to know. Trust me," he groaned as she kissed his neck.

She leaned in to whisper in his ear, "I want to know everything."

He set his head back against the carriage wall, closing his eyes. Pain crossed his features, and she clasped his cheek, needing him to say something.

"Tell me, Grady," she said, using his given name without consent. "You will not shock me. I promise."

He laughed, opening his eyes to meet hers. "You want to know what I want to do with you in this carriage?" He shook his head, setting her off his lap before wrenching her back to straddle his legs.

Ashley gasped as the position set her aching core close to his bulging manhood. His hands closed over the globes of her ass, and he wrenched her against him, his manhood teasing her through her breeches.

Exquisite sensation thrummed through her core, and she pressed against him, wanting more of this marvelous new feeling he brought forth in her.

"I want to rip those breeches from your legs, feel the heat of your thighs against my cheeks as I fuck you with my mouth. I want to eat your sweet pussy until you scream my name, holding me against you while you come upon my lips."

Wetness pooled at her core, and she gaped, having no idea that such a thing was possible. Did that mean he would kiss her cunny? The thought made her rock against him.

"What else?" she begged, needing to hear more of his wicked ways. "Tell me what this feeling is that I have within me right now. Explain to me what it is that you're making me feel?"

"Do you like what I'm making you feel?" he asked her, kissing her with such exquisite slowness that her heart did not think it could last much longer.

She nodded, the possibility of lying to him beyond her reign. She would own what she now felt, this wonderful new feeling she never wanted to end. "I do, but tell me, please. What does it mean when all I want to do is be here with you? Have you touch me...everywhere," she admitted. The thought of his hands, his mouth anywhere on her person, sent her skin to tingle with expectation.

"It means that you crave me as much as I'm craving you right at this moment. Your body wants to be filled by me, have me push into you, claim you as we want." A pained expression crossed his features before he blinked, and it was gone. "It means you want to fuck me as much as I want to fuck you. I want to thrust into your sweet, tight cunny. Let you ride me until we both spend. The need that tortures you right now is the same as mine."

Ashley bit her lip, the idea of all that he taunted her with beyond her reach.

"I want to touch you here," he whispered against her lips, the feel of his fingers grazing across her sex, the breeches she wore the only barrier between them. "I can feel your dampness. You're ready for me."

She nodded, knowing she was. "Touch me. Please," she begged him.

His hand slipped over her aching core, cupping her, his thumb circling a place on her body that ached for his touch.

"Oh, Grady, that feels wonderful," she sighed, wrapping her arms around his neck. "What are you doing to me?"

"Making you come. This is what it should be like for a woman when she's with a man. Satisfying and utterly delectable. Just as you are, a mouthwatering little minx who's corrupted me more than I already was," he said.

Ashley enjoyed knowing he was floundering as much as she was. Whenever she was around him, she lost herself in his eyes. All she wanted was to be with him, enjoy his banter, even if he was dark and scolding more often than not.

But with her, he was different. Now, with him in her arms, she knew he had a softer side. A side he kept hidden away from everyone. How long had he lived without such passion? Without happiness?

"You cannot tell me you do not like my corruption." She met his eye and saw the laughter within his.

"I should not want you anywhere near me. I'm not a good man, and my touching you here," he said, teasing her further and eliciting a moan from her, "is proof of that."

"I like that you are touching me," she gasped. "I want you to touch me a lot more than that," she admitted, unsure how she could be so bold and say such things. But something within her changed when she was around Grady Kolten, and that change was something she liked. Something she knew she wanted, not just now, but always.

## CHAPTER
# FOURTEEN

G rady worked the next few days and tried to keep the menacing minx Ashley Woodville from his mind. But it was no use. Nothing could keep her from his thoughts. Not his ministrations at the gaming hell or when he traveled to visit his mother. She haunted him, more than ever now that he'd had his first taste of her.

She intoxicated his mind, body, and soul.

He ran a hand through his hair as his mother poured him a cup of tea, dismissing the footman who remained in the room to serve them.

"I know something is bothering you, Grady. Tell me what it is, for I do not think I can stand watching you another moment squirm on your chair," she said.

He chuckled at his mother's insight. She was still a beautiful woman, even in her sixth and fiftieth year. Her hair remained dark, although there were a few silvery strands that glistened in the daylight. For her ostracized life that she had suffered due to her husband's lack of insight, the pressures on her had not lined her face, and she looked far younger than she was.

"Am I that obvious?" he asked, having always told his mother of his life and never hiding anything from her.

"What has happened? Has Blackhaven been causing you trouble? Do you need me to write to him?" she asked.

He glanced up, having not known they were even in contact. "You do not need to do that on my behalf. Father knows better than to step into my world and start throwing around his might."

His mother studied him, her eyes narrowing in thought. "Then what is bothering you? It is not like you to visit me in the middle of the week. I was not expecting you at all this fortnight."

That was all true, but he needed to speak to someone, and the only person he trusted was his mother. "There is a lady, a woman whom I have been spending time with, but I need to end the friendship. My life does not fit in with hers, and her family would never allow her to marry a man such as myself."

His mother placed down her cup and saucer with a clatter. "What do you mean by such falsehoods? You're an earl and future duke when Blackhaven takes his last breath. What lady would not look to you as a good match? They would be a simpleton indeed if they did not," she said. "You may own a gaming hell, but many gentlemen enjoy such venues. There is no shame in what you do, even if a little unconventional."

"I do not want to circulate in that world. I never have, not after it chewed you up and spat you out as if you were not worthy of any respect. She is a sister to a duchess, a marchioness, and a viscountess. There is no way that I could keep myself removed should I offer, and she accepts my hand."

His mother leaned back in her chair, studying him. "If

you cannot see yourself reentering society for her, then that is because you do not love her, and marriage would be a mistake, and I would warn you against offering for her hand. But if you have feelings for her, ones that will not be repressed, then maybe she is worth returning to the *ton* and taking your place among those you are equal to in all ways."

His mother always made sense and left him with more insight than he had when he arrived.

"Lord Walsh is sniffing about her skirts too. No matter what I do regarding offering for her hand, I shall not allow her to marry into his family."

Grady looked up and did not miss his mother's surprise at his statement.

"What the Marquess of Gibson did to me should not be pushed on to his son, Grady. You must let it go, for there is no use allowing such wounds to fester. I know from experience that life is better spent doing other things than trying to change or hating a past that we cannot alter."

Grady took a calming breath, hating to discuss the matter with his mother but knowing he needed to do so. "Lord Walsh is as bad as his father is, do not get them confused or feel sorry for the marquess's offspring. I will protect the lady I speak of, even if I do not offer marriage. She will marry a man who will love and respect her as she deserves. If she were to marry Lord Walsh, her life would be an endless cesspit of hell."

"Surely, Lord Walsh is not as bad as his father. Few could be as evil as that man," his mother admitted.

Grady knew one. His father was just as evil as the marquess, maybe due to different reasons, but still, they were the same when it came to being an honorable gentleman.

"I know things of him that prove otherwise. My gaming

hell has provided more than ample insight. Nevertheless, I thank you for allowing me to discuss my troubles today."

"You are always welcome here to discuss anything troubling you." His mother picked up her tea and took a sip. "Have I been of any help? Do you think you feel for this young mystery woman, whom you have not told me of her name, more than friendship? Has my son finally met his match?" she asked, grinning.

"Maybe," he admitted. "But I would have to change so much of myself to be with her that I'm unsure that is possible now. She has so many plans to help people, not to mention I'm certain she wishes to have a family. I never saw any of that in my life. I do not know what I feel or what I should do."

"Well," his mother said, reaching out to take his hand. "Do not leave your decision for too long. She sounds like a wonderful young woman, and such diamonds are not often seen in our society. It will not be long before others see her for the gem she is and want her for themselves. Do not lose her before you have decided if you want her or not. You will only have yourself to blame if that occurs, which is torture I never wish to see you endure. To love someone who does not love you back is a veritable nightmare."

Grady knew she was speaking of her pain regarding his sire, the current Duke of Blackhaven. The bastard had cast her out without listening to reason. His mother, the poor soul, still loved her husband, not that the duke deserved any affection.

He deserved as much as Lord Walsh, and he would not see another honest, vibrant soul like his mother's destroyed by a bad match. Even if that match were not with him, it would certainly not be with Lord Walsh.

. . .

Ashley sat in the carriage opposite Grady and patiently waited until they arrived at the orphanage near Cheapside that they were visiting. The center for the unfortunate, orphaned children was always in need of funding, and it was where Ashley wanted to help if at all possible.

Not that the orphanage would know of her just yet since she was dressed as a man. Grady suggested she change when she had arrived at his gaming hell just in case someone spotted her in the more unfashionable part of town.

Not that Ashley minded being seen for doing such charitable work, but since she would need the *ton* and its money to fund the work she wished to do here and in other locations, too, she thought it better not to scandalize anyone should they see her with the Earl of Howley, a man himself ostracised by the *ton*.

The vehicle rolled to a stop before a rundown building that several children played out in front of, their tattered clothing and dirty faces telling of the conditions within.

She jumped down onto the pavement, not waiting for Grady to open the door. She was playing a man, after all, and did not require his help.

Some of the children stopped playing with the small ball they held and watched as they made their way toward the door.

No more than five years of age, a small girl ran up to Grady and took his hand.

"Hello, Cynthia. How is my favorite girl today?" he asked.

Ashley closed her mouth shut with a snap, having not

known that Grady knew of this center or the children who lived within it.

"Very well, thank you, my lord. I have learned my numbers up to ten and my ABCs."

He tweaked her nose, smiling, and Ashley's heart thumped hard at the sight. She did not know much about the man before her, and to see him with the small girl, proud and happy for her accomplishments, had not been what she expected upon coming here.

"Will you introduce me?" Ashley asked, dipping her voice to sound more masculine.

"Of course," Grady said. "This is Miss Cynthia Smith. She's lived at the orphanage from one year of age."

"My mama died, and there was no one around to care for me," she stated without shame. Ashley smiled, but her heart ached for such children. Life was so hard and made more challenging still when there was no one to care for them.

"I'm pleased to meet you," she said.

An older woman came to the door and invited them into the building, greeting Grady with warmth. They were shown the sleeping quarters, the small school rooms, and the dining area. There were very few toys, and the beds looked in need of blankets.

"I understand from Lord Howley that you're looking to support our cause here," Mrs. Davies stated. "We are very happy to receive the support, and thank you very much if you're able to help us with funding."

"I will do all that I can," Ashley said, noting that the little girl Cynthia held on to Grady's hand and would not let him go, no matter where they went within the building.

They spoke for a time of the number of children who come into the orphanage's care. How the education was progressing for those, who took the opportunity to learn. What sort of outcome did the children expect once leaving.

None of the figures were promising, and Ashley knew poverty often reproduced more poverty for those brought up in such dire circumstances and that it was a hard burden to break free of.

Not without help.

"I have friends who are influential in London. I'm certain that we can do much more to help your organization and others like you. We, the people, owe you a great debt for caring for those who cannot care for themselves."

The older woman's eyes glistened at the compliment and she gushed nonsensical words as she tried to gain her composure. "You're too kind, and thank you. It is not inexpensive or easy doing what we do here, and we would like to see all the children who pass through our doors leave with a brighter future than the one they started with."

They spent the remainder of their visit with the children, talking to them and finding out what they wanted for themselves. Most wanted to know how to write and add and acquire jobs that would give them stability and safety in this big, unforgiving city.

On their travels back to the hell, Ashley pulled the blond wig from her hair and stared at Grady. He was pensive. His attention fixed on the window.

"You did not tell me you were acquainted with the orphanage. Why did you not say anything?" she asked, playing with the hair of her wig, which sat in her lap.

He shrugged. "Not many people take an interest in such things. That you do was a surprise and one of the reasons I agreed to help you. I knew you would do all that you threatened, no matter if I helped or not. But such orphanages do need more help, and you're a much better ally than foe, so I chose the former."

Ashley grinned. "It is good that you're seeing sense, my lord. And I will help, I guarantee it."

He did look at her then, and the affection she read in his green eyes almost made her leave her seat to sit beside him, but she did not. Not today. It was not the time, but soon she would see him again. She just needed to decide what they would do next.

The time would drag until she was with him again, as it had since the last time she had left him.

CHAPTER

# FIFTEEN

The footman in his liveried attire bade them welcome as they entered Whites. Tonight Grady had agreed to show her one of London's most exclusive gentlemen's clubs.

She was a woman dressed as a gentleman and would see for herself where so many men congregated and enjoyed their own private hideaway from the debutantes and marriage-obsessed mamas of the *ton*. It was something she had longed to see.

The men so often ridiculed the ladies for their feminine wiles, their like of Almacks, of gossip and such, but did they not do the same here at Whites. There was the famous betting book of course, which proved the point they enjoyed gossip and knew what society was always about. Tonight she would see for herself what this exclusive men's club was like and she all but burst with excitement to get inside.

Ashley followed Grady up the stairs, and they came to a large coffee room that overlooked the street. Tonight there were few in attendance, only a scattering of members. No doubt due to the Cavendish ball that anyone who was anyone would attend.

Her sisters were all there, and again Ashley had pleaded exhaustion to remain home. She would not get away with such excuses for much longer. They would think she was ill and send her home, and that would never do.

Grady walked to a small table surrounded by four chairs, and they sat. A footman promptly came over and took their orders.

"What would you like this evening, my lord?" the young man asked her.

Ashley thought on the matter a moment, having never had an order taken from her like this before. It was a novel experience. "A beer, please," she said.

Grady smiled across from her before ordering a brandy. The footman left, and Grady met her eyes. "A beer, Ash. Have you ever had one before?"

Ashley shrugged, looking about and settling farther into the leather chair. The room was opulent, the Aubusson rug underneath her feet thick and soft. Books were in several bookcases, the color scheme of the room masculine and dark. "No, but I have seen my father drink it a time or two, and he seems to enjoy it very much. I'm certain I will be the same," she answered, looking to the door when a group of young bucks she had not seen before walked into the club.

"Ignore anyone who comes and keep your attention on me or the paper on the table before us. Do not try to bring attention to yourself if you can help it. You're still utterly fetching and feminine for all your clothing and boyish haircut."

Ashley leaned forward to ensure privacy. "Are you

telling me, Lord Howley, that you find a gentleman handsome? And handsome enough to tempt you?"

The salacious look he gave her made her shiver. "Had I not known you were a woman under those clothes, then yes, I will admit I would have studied you further. But those high cheekbones and your skin soon give you away. Not a whisker in sight, and no Adam's apple either."

Ashley swallowed and pulled up her cravat to cover more of her neck. "Well, it has fooled enough people so far, and that is all that I need my disguise to do. And in any case," she added, "I do not want anyone else looking at me with interest."

"Really?" he drawled, thanking the footman as he set down their drinks, leaving them yet again. "Tell me who you would like to look at you."

Ashley met his eye and hoped he could read all the wants and needs she felt for the man sitting across from her. She wanted him, all of him, if only he would give her more of what he had already given her a taste of.

"Wouldn't you like to know," she teased.

"Yes," he said, gesturing to her drink. "Have your beer, and then I shall show you around. We cannot stay long. The night's entertainments will only keep the gentlemen away for so long, and I do not want you here when it is busy."

She picked up her glass and took a sip. The bitter, flat brew made her stomach curdle, and she fought not to spit it out. "Urgh, it is disgusting. Why did you not tell me how awful my choice was?" she asked him accusingly.

He shrugged, sipping his brandy. "It was much more amusing to watch you try something new. Sometimes when we experience something we have never partaken in before, it can be a pleasurable, enjoyable, worthwhile."

Ashley narrowed her eyes, having the distinct feeling he

was no longer talking of beverages. She picked up the beer again, determined to drink it down if only to say she had tried it in full and found it wanting.

The beverage did not go down easily, but they both finished their drinks over the next few minutes. "How about that tour?" she suggested.

He untangled his legs and stood. Ashley followed him, and he showed her the back dining hall central to the building. A small hall led off from there that brought them back to the staircase. A room at the rear of the building was reserved for cards and gambling.

They then headed back downstairs, entering the main hall. The two front rooms that looked out onto the street were divided by the main hall on this level. Where the card room was upstairs, downstairs a billiard room took pride of place.

Just as they were heading back to the main hall, the doors to the club opened, and in walked Lord Walsh and Lord Fenton. They handed over their coats to a waiting footman, and without warning, Grady pushed her into a small room under the stairs.

The little amount of light that filtered in showed the small space to have a desk and other items, a bucket, and cloths. A cleaning storage room, perhaps. Grady remained at the door, listening to what Lord Walsh was stating in the foyer.

"I do not think he saw us," she whispered, feeling her way to the desk before sitting on it. She swung her legs, a small grin lifting her lips as Grady persisted in keeping guard.

The moment boots scuffed the steps of the stairs, only then did he join her at the desk. He stood before her, tall and masculine, and heat pooled at her core.

After their night in the carriage from Vauxhall, she knew she wanted him again. Wanted to feel what he could do to her.

"What are you thinking?" she asked him, reaching boldly out to clasp his superfine coat.

"You do not want to know," he answered in a low and gravelly tone.

Oh yes, she did want to know. "Do you want to know what I'm thinking?" she queried.

He stepped closer when she pulled him toward her. "Always," he said.

"Well, I want you to kiss me again."

G rady needed no further urging to do as she wished. He took her lips in a searing kiss, her delightful sigh as their tongues tangled making him hard.

He could not take her here—Whites of all places—but nor could he drag himself away from her sweet mouth.

Her hands were everywhere upon him, touching him, slipping under his shirt, dipping to his ass, pulling him to nestle between her thighs.

He could not help himself. He took the opportunity to rub against her sex, their breeches the only thing keeping him from taking her.

He was certain she would have him too, but she deserved far better than a quick tup under the stairs at a gentlemen's club. She deserved silk and flowers, champagne, and a bed fit for the queen.

His queen.

"Oh, Grady," she moaned, rolling her hips against him.

"You like that?" he asked her.

"Yes," she sighed. "You madden me with need. I cannot

get enough of you," she said.

He could not seem to get enough of her either. Something he realized with growing concern. She was a lady, and he was as far from a gentleman if ever there was one. They could not be together, not unless they both sacrificed things in their life he was not sure they could.

Grady guided her hips, helping her ride him through his clothes. He had never come this way before in his life, but by God, he wanted to, right at this moment.

She was flushed, her sweet bottom lip clasped beneath her teeth. He wanted to rip her breeches down and impale her with his cock.

The thought made his balls tighten, and he knew he would soon spend.

Ashley made sweet, gasping moans, throwing her head back, heedless of where they were.

"Oh yes, Grady," she sighed.

The sound of men's laughter pulled him to his senses, and he stilled as footsteps into the billiards room sounded outside.

Ashley, too, held still, the two of them holding their breath as the danger passed. "We need to go," he said, not giving her a chance to change his mind.

Before leaving, he pulled her from the desk and quickly checked how presentable she was. He strode for the main doors, not looking at anyone who may be about as Ashley followed close on his heels.

He would return her home, safe and sound, and no harm done. Except he knew the damage that she had caused him. Somehow, she had managed to also venture under his skin in her excursions. And now, he could not refuse her anything.

Not even himself.

# CHAPTER
# SIXTEEN

"So you see, Hailey, this is the perfect charity you ought to give to and help me raise funds. You're a duchess now. People do expect you to help others, you know," Ashley pushed, trying to pick her words carefully so her sister would assist her.

They were home this morning and expecting callers. Hailey set down her cup of tea, sighing at her continued mentioning of the orphanage. "And how do you know of this orphanage? I hope you have not been traveling anywhere you should not, and unaccompanied. You know London is not safe, and it is certainly a lot different from Grafton. You cannot travel about the same."

Ashley waved her concerns aside just as the butler announced the first of several guests. "I have not, but through friends, I have learned of this orphanage, and I think we need to help in any way we can. They need toys and clothing for the children, not to mention bedding before the winter months. Please help me," she begged.

Hailey stared at her a moment before she nodded. "Very

well. Of course, I shall help, and we will discuss it further when we're not busy hosting guests."

Ashley nodded, smiling at her sister just as Lord Walsh bowed before her, taking her hand and kissing it. A shiver of revulsion ran through her before he seated himself at her side.

Ashley adjusted her seat, taking the opportunity to move a little away from his lordship. "Lord Walsh, so good of you to call."

"It is, is it not?" he answered. "I have been meaning to for several days, but today, your lucky day as it was, I thought I should finally come and speak to you."

Ashley did not comment, merely waited for the footman to pour Lord Walsh a cup of tea. "How very fortunate for us for you to call," she lied, Grady's warning of Lord Walsh loud in her mind. "What is it that you wished to speak to me about?"

"Well, as to that, I wanted to say how very original and bold you are. I did not think any woman of the *ton* would ever catch my eye, but you, Miss Woodville, have certainly done so."

"Really? How so?" she asked, although the smugness in his eyes told her that maybe she would prefer not to know at all.

"I saw you the other day in a carriage. You did not see me as you drove past as you were engaged in conversation within the equipage, but I certainly saw you."

Something in his words made her stomach knot, and she pasted a smile on her lips, hoping to dissuade him of anything he may have seen that could see her ruined. Depending on when his lordship had seen her, that was.

"I'm surprised you could make anyone out in a carriage, me or otherwise, my lord. The vehicles pass so quickly that one is often mistaken in who they believe in having glimpsed."

He chuckled, shaking his head. "Oh no, I was not mistaken. I saw you with Lord Howley, alone too, I might add. But the strange thing about it all was that you were wearing men's attire. I followed you, of course. I was in that part of London and had my horse readily available and caught up to you at the orphanage you were visiting. At first, I thought I had made a mistake, that it was not you visiting the premises, but then I saw you walk and I knew that it was you. The sway of your delectable hips is something that is imprinted on my mind."

Ashley swallowed, forcing herself not to react to his words, but she could do little to stop the blood draining from her face. She wanted to chastise him, give him a proper set down at his forward and rude words. How dare he think he could speak to any lady in such an underhanded manner.

Ashley calmed her racing heart and temper and fought not to give herself away. "You do make me laugh, my lord. Why would I have reason to wear men's clothing to an orphanage? Are you certain you had not imbibed too much wine that day?" she asked, trying to dissuade him of the fact.

"Oh no, it was you, alright. Lord Howley at your side, who had a wolfish look on his face, the one he gets whenever he sees a woman he wants to fuck. And since I know his tastes do not run for the male kind, it made me more than ever positive that it was you whom I saw."

Ashley had heard enough of his crudeness. She stood, and he clasped her arm, yanking her to sit. "Do not deny it. I know it was you, and I want to know why you're associating with Howley. He's an outcast, a nobody. You ought to act better considering who your sisters married. To associate with such a man will bring your family nothing but shame."

The insult against Grady irked her, and she fought not to scream back at him that he was the one who was vile and ought to be ostracised from society. His manners, such as they were today and his rude, disrespectful speech toward her showed a man nothing like the one he portrayed to the *ton*.

"You are mistaken, my lord. It was not me you saw, and there is nothing further to be said on the matter." She reached for her cup of tea, thankful her hand did not shake. "Is there anything else you wished to discuss before I take a turn about the room? Or would you like to voice more vulgar words for my hearing only?" she asked him, her voice calm and sweet. Nothing like the turmoil that rioted within her.

He wagged a finger in her face, tsk tsk-tsking her. "Oh, no, you don't, Miss Woodville. This conversation is far from over. With this knowledge, there are things that I want. Things that only you can give, and what you will agree to lest I ruin you and your sister back at Grafton, who's still to make her debut."

Fear curdled in her stomach, and she raised her chin, determined not to be blackmailed by such a creature. He could not prove anything about her. "Really, my lord. Do tell?" she asked. "I'm all ears."

"I want you to marry me. Although I know your family is mere farmers from the country, your dowries are substantial, I have heard. You will also suit my tastes, which vary from time to time, but I always enjoy brunettes. That will never change."

Ashley almost cast up her accounts at the thought of

marrying the man before her. Was he mad? She would never do as he wished.

"As I said, you're mistaken that I was with Lord Howley. I hardly know the gentleman. As you said, he rarely attends social events."

"He attended your coming out, which is proof enough if I were looking for an attachment between you two. He has not attended any *ton* event for years, not after his mother was cast out for a good reason. Do not suffer the same fate as her. I would hate for you to ruin your future merely because you had some unfounded hope of marrying Howley. He will never marry. That is one thing that is known of the man."

Ashley tried to ignore the spike of despair Lord Walsh's words prickled within her. She had secretly hoped that Grady would step back into society and want her as much as she wanted him.

Not just for the secretive outings he was helping her to enjoy, but because she wanted him as her husband. She wanted him to be the man she grew old with, maybe have children if they were so fortunate. She did not want it with the man before her.

"I'll tell you what, Miss Woodville. I shall give you a week or so to think over my proposal. But if you decide you wish to test my word on ruining you, I would suggest you do not return to me the answer that would bring forth such events."

"You're a disgraceful man. I had thought maybe what I had heard of you may be wrong, that you were not as terrible as it was being made out to me that you were. But I was mistaken and have been believing the best of someone who does not deserve it."

"You lie. No one would sully my name. I'm an

upstanding citizen of London, a catch for any young woman if I say so myself. So do be careful, Miss Woodville. If we're to marry, you do not wish to get me in a temper. That trait, I will admit, is not as pretty as my face."

Ashley stood, slapping Lord Walsh's hand away when he again attempted to keep her near. "Leave my sister's home now before I ask the duke to escort you out. You're not welcome here again."

He smirked, the disgraceful amusement in his gaze making her blood run cold. "I will send word in a week and will expect an answer from you then. Good day to you, Miss Woodville. Always a pleasure."

Ashley watched his every step as he made his way out of the room. Whatever would she do? How unfortunate it was that she had been seen with Grady, especially when they had been so careful not to be spotted.

There was only one thing for it. She would have to stop her excursions about London for the next few weeks at least. Be seen at every ball and party, so no one would believe his lies when Lord Walsh tried to tarnish her name.

She certainly could not be seen with Grady again. Not until she had overcome this troubling issue.

Ashley swallowed, blinking back the tears that threatened. She did not want to stay away from him. Right now, she wanted to run to him, have him hold her, and tell her it all would be well. That he would not let anything happen to her and that she would not be forced to marry a man she had come to loathe because of her mistake.

A mistake of her own doing.

# CHAPTER
# SEVENTEEN

Grady kicked his heels at the front of the London Museum, waiting for Ashley to arrive, and yet, two hours after their agreed meeting, she had not joined him.

When she did not send a note or explain her absence from their jaunt to Richmond, he knew there was something wrong. Or at least something had happened, and she was not telling him.

Had she grown bored by their outings? Had she found someone else to do her bidding? Had another gentleman swept her off her slippered feet? Grady leaned back in his chair behind his desk and glared at the parchment of bills from the many traders who supplied his hell.

He glanced at the clock on his mantel. It was well past ten in the evening, the *ton* events would have just started to ramp up, and it was a perfect opportunity to find Ashley and see what she was about.

He did not want to think that maybe the woman who occupied his mind day and night had formed an attachment with another gentleman and would soon be announcing a betrothal to him.

He pushed back from his desk, striding to his bedchamber and changing quickly into a superfine suit that he always kept on the ready. Tonight was the Marquess of Craig's ball, which kept many gentlemen from his doors, at least until the early-morning hours when they would stumble into his gaming hell and lose money that some did not have to lose in the first place.

He stood before his mirror, tying his cravat before striding for the door, determined to find out what had happened to Ashley. Was she well? He had not heard she was ill, but that did not mean she was not.

The carriage ride to Mayfair took several minutes, and he was soon standing at the entrance doors to the gilded room, the hundreds of guests taking no heed of his presence.

People milled about the edge of the room while others danced the Allemande. The scent of sweat and perfume permeated the air, and he cast his eyes across the sea of heads, trying to find his quarry.

And then he saw her. Standing beside Lord Walsh, her pallor, the distaste and fear that lurked in her eyes was nothing he ever wished to see on any woman, least of all Ashley.

He started toward them, not caring if his directness caused a stir. He knew he needed to be by her side and keep her safe from the vulture hovering over her like she was his next prey.

Lord Walsh spied him first, the shock registering on the bastard's face, followed by his paleness, warming the cockles of his heart.

"Lord Howley, how good of you to come. Miss Woodville," Walsh said.

Ashley's attention flew to him as if she were ready to jump into his arms and let him whisk her away from the hell she was living. Which he wasn't uncertain he was not going to do. "You remember Lord Howley, of course. I know you are acquainted."

Grady met Walsh's eyes and glared at the bastard. What was he insinuating? Was this why she had not been to see him? "Good evening, Miss Woodville. I hope you've been enjoying the Season since we last met at your coming-out ball," he reminded Walsh, not willing for any slurs to mar Ashley's reputation.

"Oh, of course, her coming out," Walsh said, his voice mocking.

Ashley dipped into a curtsy. "Very much, my lord. I did not think to see you here this evening. I hope you have come to dance?" she asked, staring at him with such hope that he could not refuse her.

He held out his hand, which she readily took. "Please, oblige me this next dance, Miss Woodville, although I must apologize for my dancing may be a little unpolished since I never partake in the activity."

"I do not mind in the least," she answered. "I would love to dance with you."

Grady pulled her onto the dance floor just as the minstrels started to play a minuet. Grady pulled her into his arms, welcoming the feel of her again. For all his denial of his feelings for the woman, he had missed her and worried for her during their time apart.

Relief poured through him that she was safe and well, and no matter the reason she had not been near him these past few days, nothing could be as bad as not being together as they had been.

"Where have you been? You did not attend the London Museum or the ride to Richmond as agreed. I had to come to find you and ensure all was well."

"I'm sorry, my lord," she said, staring down at the ground before she cast a quick glance toward Lord Walsh, who continued to watch them.

"I cannot partake in our excursions any longer, although I will, of course, help the orphanage as agreed. I already have my sister, the duchess helping me with funding."

"I do not care about any of that. I know you will keep your word, but why have you not been to see me?" he asked, hating that he sounded like a lovesick fool who could not live without the woman in his arms.

He wasn't uncertain he was not that man.

*My God, what have I become*, he wondered as he waited for her reply.

T*ell him, Ashley.* The words banged about in her mind, and she knew she ought to tell Grady what Lord Walsh was threatening her. He would help her, stop the menace or at least know what was to be done.

She glanced up at him, the concern on his visage almost breaking her resolve to remain quiet.

She could not tell him. She had dragged him into her games as it was when he had never asked to be involved in the first place. He had never wanted to take her about London, show her all that she could not learn and see without his help.

"Lord Walsh is nothing but a pest that will soon tire of

me and look for another. There is nothing wrong. I merely have seen all that I wished to of London and no longer need your assistance."

"Really?" he drawled, his words mocking as if he did not believe her, and he ought not to. Nothing of what she said was true. "Why do I feel you're not telling me the truth? There is more as to why you have not come to see me. I know there is. You cannot be as passionate, feel what I thought you did in my arms, and then cut me off as if I do not matter to you."

She met his eyes and swallowed hard. She could not marry the man before her. He was everything that she had been warned to stay away from, and yet, to marry Lord Walsh, a wolf who paraded about as if butter would not melt in his mouth, was far worse.

Grady had never threatened her, bullied, or tried to take advantage of her. He was kind, attentive, and so passionate. He may not be part of fashionable London, but that did not make him any less appealing. If anything, it made him more so.

"We are friends, and I thank you truly for showing me the London I would not otherwise know, but to read more into what has been happening between us is a mistake you ought to correct within yourself."

"Wow," he said, pulling her to the side of the room and stepping away from her. "I had not thought you could be cold, Miss Woodville, but it would seem that I'm mistaken."

She nodded, looking past Grady to see Lord Walsh smirking at her from several feet away. "I'm not cold, I like you very much as a friend, but you must not believe more than that. I know you are not the marrying kind. You would have to be blind not to see that for yourself. And that is your choice which I will not try to sway. You're an active man, and my pestering you to take me all about London is a hindrance. I ought to have known better. I will not shadow your door again."

He bowed, the hard lines of his face making her want to squirm under his inspection of her. Did he know she was lying? Did he want to call her out for her falsehoods?

"See that you do not," he barked, his words cutting her to her core before he turned and strode away. Ashley watched him disappear out of the ballroom doors, wanting to go after him. She wanted to tell him the truth. But as a gentleman, far more honorable than Lord Walsh, Lord Howley would feel the need to offer marriage if what was known of her became a rumor in the *ton*.

She did not want any man to marry her out of duty and not love.

She glared at Lord Walsh and moved toward her sister Hailey, wanting to return home and away from the vicious *ton*.

Away from a man she loathed more with every breath. At home, at least, she did not have to tolerate him or listen to his threats.

CHAPTER

# EIGHTEEN

Ashley spent the next three days in agony. The words she had said to Grady tormented her. No matter if she were at a ball or dinner party, nothing stopped her from thinking of what she had told him. The lies she had spoken.

She sat in a hackney cab, dressed as a man as she often was when traveling to the East End. She would see Grady and make him listen to her so she could tell him the truth. She would apologize and ask for help.

He would know how she could rid herself of Lord Walsh, who seemed more determined than ever to make trouble for her. The carriage rocked to a halt, and she jumped down, throwing the driver a silver coin before starting for the back entrance to the gaming hell.

Dressed as she was, she knew she could enter through the main doors, but she needed to see Grady alone. She could not risk Walsh being here and seeing her yet again visiting a man unchaperoned in the middle of the night.

She passed several workers who threw her interested glances as she strode by them, heading for the door. Why none of them asked what she was about was curious, and she couldn't help but wonder if Grady had told them of his friend Ash who was welcome here.

Ashley took the stairs and came to a skidding halt at the door of Grady's office. He sat in his chair, leaning back and grinning up at the woman who sat on his desk facing him.

She swallowed the bile that rose in her throat, and the shocked gasp, which to her mortification was utterly feminine, not masculine as she was portraying, slipped past her lips.

Grady's attention snapped to the door, and he stood, his chair slamming into the wall at his back.

"Mr. Ash," he said, using her alias.

The woman on his desk turned to look at her, and there must have been something about Ashley that gave her away, for the woman's smirk soon slipped from her painted face and turned into a scowl.

"What are you doing here?" he asked, coming around his desk.

Ashley watched, transfixed, as the woman slipped from his desk and sauntered about the room to the fire where she stayed and warmed herself. Her gown, or what was left of it, hung from her, leaving little to men's imagination.

"Apologies. I see you're busy." Ashley fled down the hall as fast as her feet would carry her.

What was she doing here? Of course, he had a life before she had involved herself in it. She knew he was the type of man to have a lover, if not lovers. Why she would think herself superior to his past, she had little idea. A diversion that would make him give up all he had before. She had been deluding herself, and she should not be here. Tears flooded her eyes, and she increased her pace, needing to get away before he saw how upset the scene made her.

A warm, strong hand wrapped about her arm and pulled her to a stop just as she made the stairs.

"Oh no, you do not," Grady growled behind her, dragging her into a room she had not been in before. It was as opulent as the ducal suite at her sister's home, and for a moment, she stood stupefied, taking in the grandeur.

"This is your room? Here?" she managed to say, unable to find the words to say what her mind was seeing. A large four-poster bed with rich, blue velvet bedding set against one wall, a large marble fireplace burned and gave the room a warmth lacking from its master's visage at this very moment. He had a desk in here, too, covered in papers and a golden quill that would have been perfect for stealing during her first foray to his den.

She crossed her arms and raised her chin. Anger thrummed through her that she had seen him with another woman and looked delighted about that fact. The thought made her eyes burn further, and she fought not to sob.

"Yes," he said, snicking the lock on the door and walking past her to move to the fire. He turned to stare at her. His mouth pinched into a displeased line. "I thought you would be at some ball or dinner this evening. Word has it that you'll soon be engaged to Walsh. I ought to offer my congratulations, but commiserations I think would be better suited."

She shook her head. Had Lord Walsh spread such lies about his intentions over London? Did people think she was eager to be his wife? Mortification swamped her, and heat kissed her cheeks.

"I was at a ball. I left. I needed to see you," she admitted. "To explain why I need to distance myself from you."

He raised his brows, his strong jaw and chiseled cheeks seemingly more menacing under the firelight of his room.

"Do explain, Miss Woodville," he asked her, his eyes burning with hurt and disappointment. Both emotions were something she had done and not proudly so.

She came up to him, needing to be near him. "Lord Walsh has seen me with you. Although I have not admitted to his accusations, he is threatening to tell everyone of what he's seen unless I marry him."

"What?" he barked. "The hell he is." Grady clasped her upper arms and shook her a little. "What did the bastard say exactly? I need to know before I kill him."

Ashley relayed her conversation with Lord Walsh, word for word, and the murderous look on Grady's face left a cold shiver down her spine.

"Why did you not tell me?" he said, pulling her to sit on a nearby daybed. "I would have put a stop to his threats. He cannot prove a thing, and he has nothing if you do not own up to them."

"I know that, and I haven't said a word, but I felt as though I was as bad as he was and could not tell you the truth. I forced you into my mess. I manipulated your conscience into helping me galivant about London. Even knowing the bachelor lifestyle you lead and that it would be unlikely you would offer marriage, a union I would need if I was ever caught." She shrugged, at a loss as to what to do. "If Lord Walsh follows through on his threat, I did not want you forced into offering for me." Ashley slumped her head into her hands. "I'm so sorry to bring so much trouble." She stood, needing to go. "You seemed busy when I arrived, and I have intruded yet again. I should leave. I just wanted you to know why I cannot see you anymore."

. . .

The hell he would not see her again. Grady pulled her back down on the daybed, not wanting her to go anywhere. He was not sure what was happening to him whenever he was around Ashley, but he knew that not being with her was worse than anything else.

He was an outcast in society. Her family would never approve of him, especially as his father made no secret of his belief that Grady was not even legitimate.

It was a lie, debunked by many, but still, the shadow lurked, and he doubted Ashley's family would want to have that shadow follow her—or any children they made —around.

Even so, he could not let her leave. Could not let her think he did not want to help or be with her as much as he could.

"I was not busy at all," he lied, knowing his mistress was trying, very unsuccessfully, he may add, to get him into her bed. He had allowed her flirting but nothing more. The thought of bedding anyone brought no allure, not if that anyone was not the woman sitting before him.

"But the lady in your office. I should not have intruded," she said again.

Grady lifted her chin to meet her eyes, needing to see her lovely face. "The lady is in my past, Ashley," he admitted, not sure why he was so honest when it came to her. "If I wanted to be with her, I would not have chased after you out of my office as if the hounds of hell were nipping at my boots."

She threw him a small smile, hope lighting her eyes for the first time that night. "I need to admit something to you," she said.

"What?" he replied, drinking in her pretty face as he waited for her to find the nerve to say what she must.

"When I forced you into helping me have my nights out in London, it was because the very first time that I saw you, I wanted you for myself. And when you kissed me in the carriage, I knew I would never be able to walk away from you."

Grady slipped his hand about her nape, pulling her close. He bent his head, sighing in part pleasure and relief at kissing her once more. She was home to him, sweetness and fire all wrapped up in a delicious, lovely bundle that was Ashley Woodville.

Their tongues tangled, and she shuffled nearer, her hands fisting upon the lapels of his coat. "Give me this night, Grady," she asked. "Give me one last request of you."

Last? He'd be damned if this would be the last time he had her in his arms. "I will give you all that I can, Ashley," he said, loving the sound of her name on his lips. He kissed her again, pleasure thrumming through him, hot and wild, unlike anything he'd ever experienced before.

He fumbled with her jacket and shirt, having never undressed another man before. She did not shy away from his touch. Her fingers mixed with his as they shed their clothes.

He ought not to live up to the rake he was, but nothing, not even another scandal in the many of his life, could stop him from having her. Of giving her what she wanted.

Tonight would be the first, but not the last.

## CHAPTER

# NINETEEN

Nerves skittled across her skin as Grady rid her of her clothing. Her own hands were busy with removing his waistcoat and shirt. He wore no cravat, and the sight of his chest, the scattering of dark hairs, left her breathless.

She had never seen a man naked before, and although he still wore his breeches, she knew she would soon see all of him, every delicious bit of his body.

Ashley reached out, running her hand over his chest. The muscles jerked beneath her touch. He was warm, his breathing as labored as hers.

"You're so muscular," she said, biting her lip and enjoying her little tour of his body.

"You're so beautiful," he said, pulling the wig from her head. Her hair spilled down over her shoulders. In her haste to see him, she had not braided and pinned it down.

Ashley kneeled on the daybed and pushed Grady down onto the many cushions about them. "I want to be with you so much," she admitted, leaning over to kiss him. She moaned as his hands came about her waist and slid over her bottom, squeezing her.

"I want to be with you too," he said. He reached for her falls and ripped the buttons open, sliding her breeches down her legs. Ashley helped him with his endeavors and kicked them the rest of the way off.

He rolled over her, pinning her beneath him, and she wrapped her legs about his waist. The feeling of him over her, his warmth and strength, the feel of his engorged manhood pressing against her sex was too much. She could not wait too much longer.

She did as he and ripped his falls open. Grady moved off the daybed, towering over her as he pushed his breeches down. Ashley sighed, her attention moving from his handsome face to his muscular chest. His eyes promised wicked, lovely things that she was yet to learn.

Her gaze dipped to the V at the base of his stomach to the protruding, heavy cock that stood to attention.

Her attention, a wicked part of her mind crowed.

He was reminiscent of a Greek god, magnificent and virile.

Grady kneeled at the edge of the daybed, his eyes glistening with wickedness that she had never seen before.

He wrenched her closer, and Ashley yelped before stilling as his mouth kissed its way along her inner thigh.

She swallowed, tried to relax, and stared at the ceiling as she waited for what he would do. Heat crept across her face, and she was glad that he could not see her embarrassment.

The feel of his tongue circling the sensitive skin on her thigh made her ache, and she stilled, waiting for what he would do next. Hoping that what she imagined him doing would come to fruition.

Small, soft kisses brushed her mons, and she moaned, letting her legs fall open, letting him have at her as much as they both wanted.

"You're a sweet hellion," he murmured before his tongue slipped across her sex, teasing her, kissing her with relentless strokes. "I cannot get enough of you," he admitted.

Ashley moaned, her hands reaching down to hold his head where he made love to her with his mouth, not wanting him to ever move from his wicked ministrations.

His mouth kissed her, suckled, and teased her. Up and down, he kissed before the pressure of a finger circled the outside of her sex.

"Grady, yes, please, yes," she murmured, her world spinning out of control.

"You like me fucking you with my mouth?" he asked her, his crude words only adding to her enjoyment.

"Yes, yes, I do," she admitted.

He slowly pushed one finger into her wet, aching flesh, and stars floated behind her eyelids. He mimicked what she assumed a man's phallus would do with his finger. With the ministrations of his mouth, his tongue, heat coursed through every part of her.

Her body felt alive, on fire, needy and greedy for more. He worked her, made love to her with his mouth, and it was too much. The sensation he had wrought within her in the carriage tingled through her blood.

She closed her eyes, and allowed the sensations to grow, bloom, and erupt.

And then they did.

Pleasure rocked through her. Grady groaned against her sex, his hand and mouth working her to a frenzy. "Grady," she screamed, holding him against her like a wanton, undone by how he made her feel and not caring how she would be perceived so long as he did not stop.

As her pleasure ebbed, he came over her, positioning himself at her core. "Are you sure?" he asked, the feel of his cock, hard and huge at her opening, no longer as scary as it had been.

Now the thought of having him in her, taking her as they both wished, was a desire she did not want to wait on for another second.

"I'm sure. Please, I want you," she said.

He slid into her, her wetness, the sensation of her orgasm extending her pleasure. She could not get enough of him. How would she walk away now, after what they had shared tonight?

He kissed her. Hard. His mouth demanded a response she was happy to give. Ashley wrapped herself about him, holding him as he took her with relentless, unforgiving strokes. They did not make love. This was far too fast, too hard and furious for such sentiments. He owned her, marked her with his touch, and pushed her to heights she had never climbed before.

"Ashley," he groaned, their tongues tangling, their bodies one.

"Grady," she whispered back, meeting his eyes.

He watched her, took her, and something inside her changed. A sensation and feeling unlike any she had ever known thrummed through her, and she knew her life would never be the same after tonight.

And she hoped that it was not. For a life without Grady was no life at all. How would she convince him? That she did not know, but she knew she would try. Her future happiness depended on it.

· · ·

Grady paced his office the following evening. After having escorted Ashley home in the early hours of the morning. Before her sister and the duke had returned from the evening's entertainments. He could not wait to see her again.

He was not used to feeling the novel emotion, but it was one he could get used to. The sound of a carriage caught his attention, and he glanced down at the delivery yard. He had instructed his driver to drop her off and smiled at the sight of Ashley alighting from the carriage.

Her movements were careful and ladylike, nothing like the men's clothing she wore.

He started across the room, headed for the stairs, and met her halfway up. Without the patience to wait another moment, he pulled her into his arms, kissing her soundly.

She was warm, welcoming, and passionate, and his body roared with the need for her. With the presence of mind to keep her safe always.

"Are you ready for our adventure?" he asked her, taking her hand and starting back down the stairs to the carriage outside.

"Yes, but you have not told me where we're going. Am I dressed suitably?" she asked him.

He nodded, letting go of her hand before they entered the courtyard, lest any of his workers saw him holding the hand of a young male. Not the type of scandal he wanted to be embroiled in. It was bad enough should he be caught with an heiress, an unmarried debutante, without adding more fuel to the fire they created.

He opened the door and watched as she stepped up into the carriage. The sight of her round, pert ass made his mouth water, and his hands itch to touch it.

Grady followed her and tapped the roof, signaling to his driver to leave. "I thought this evening we ought to do something relatively alone."

She tipped her head to the side, throwing him a quizzical glance. "That is not at all helpful, Grady. Tell me where we're going?" she asked him, sitting beside him and taking his hand, playing with his fingers with her own.

She was so happy and lighthearted that her demeanor was infectious, and he wanted to bask in her light. Never leave the comfort that she ensured.

"It shall not take long to get there," he said, tapping her nose with his finger. "Patience, my darling."

She rolled her eyes, but her smile gave her mood away. She leaned forward, looking out the window, no doubt trying to place their location.

"We're heading toward the Thames." She turned to look at him. "Are we going on an adventure? Are you scurrying me away in the dark of night to marry me at Gretna?"

He barked out a laugh, but the idea had merit. "Would you agree to an elopement should I procure the means to have one?" he asked, unsure where the odd proposal came from, but not regretting it.

She huddled up to his side, meeting his eye. "I would go anywhere with you. You only need to ask," she said, hope and expectation burning in her beautiful brown eyes.

The carriage rolled to a halt, and seemingly forgetting all about their conversation, Ashley jumped toward the door, looking to see where they were.

"We're at the Thames," she said, her voice unsure.

"Yes, and now our adventure begins."

## CHAPTER
# TWENTY

Ashley opened the carriage door before Grady could for her and jumped down. She looked about and tried to see what the adventure her beloved had organized for the night would be.

The sound of lapping water filled the night air, along with laughter and music. She turned about and spied a tavern a little along the dock. Grady came up to her, gesturing her toward stairs that led down to the water's edge.

"Is it safe?" she asked, moving to stand at the top. The stairs were dark, with only the moonlight on the water giving light to where he wanted her to go.

"Of course it is." He whistled, and a lamp appeared at the base of the stairs, a man holding it aloft to help them find their footing.

Grady took her arm and helped her make her way down. Nerves and excitement converged in her belly. She had never been on the Thames before, although she had seen people working on it when they came and went from London.

"This is our adventure." Grady nodded in welcome to the older man who stood at the back of the Venetian boat. The area the occupants sat in was covered by whimsically draped cloth, giving them privacy from the man who steered the vessel.

Pillows lay everywhere, along with a bottle of wine and two flutes for their use. The seating gave them a view of the stars and London on this pretty and balmy evening.

Never in her life had Ashley seen anything so romantic.

Grady assisted her onto the boat before helping her to sit. He joined her, settling himself beside her. She looked around. All of London bustled about them, but here on the water, they were alone, secluded and safe from prying eyes.

"Wait," she said, meeting Grady's eye. "Will there not be talk of you escorting a young man to a boat made for seduction?" she asked him, not wanting him to get into trouble.

"No." He shook his head. "My carriage driver and the boatman both know me, and I have explained the situation. There is no fear to be had," he explained.

"Very well. I'm satisfied," she said, excitement bubbling up in her for their night alone.

"So surprise, my darling Ashley," he said, reaching out to slip the wig from her head. "You're so beautiful. You make my heart ache."

She grinned, laying back with Grady, unable to remove the smile from her lips. "You're such a flatterer. I hope you do not tell all the ladies such words," she teased.

"Only when they're alone with me like this." She pinched his stomach, and he barked out a laugh, yelping when she did it again.

"Take that back before I dive into the water and leave you forever," she warned him.

He continued to laugh, making her lips twitch. "Very well. I take it back." He cupped her face, meeting her eyes. "You must know that I have never said any such words to anyone but you."

She shivered, pleased that he would be so open to her. She wanted a love match, a man she could trust and who would trust her with all their secrets, desires, and dreams.

"You know, when we first met, I thought you wicked and hard, but in truth, you're nothing like that. Not really. I think inside that hard outer shell you carry, your heart is nothing but a beating organ of affection."

He shrugged but did not look away from her eyes. "For you, it may be so, but no one else."

Was he trying to tell her that he loved her? As they lay under the stars, the soothing sound of the water lapping at the boat would be the perfect time for a gentleman to declare such feelings for a lady.

Even so, if he did not, Ashley could not help but feel that if he did not love her, he liked her far more than anyone ever before in his life. And that was enough for her.

For now.

"There is more to my night under the stars," he said, sitting up and dragging a basket toward them. "I thought we may have a picnic."

Ashley's stomach took that very moment to rumble, and she placed her hand atop it, laughing. "I apologize. I have not eaten since dinner, and that was several hours ago."

He chuckled, pulling out a sandwich with cucumber in it. Her favorite. "Here, this should help."

Ashley bit into the light meal and relished the taste of it. Maybe she was hungrier than she thought. She took the opportunity to watch Grady bite into a sweet, juicy strawberry and knew that as much as she welcomed food right at this time, she was more ravenous for the man at her side.

He was starting to become an addiction she could not live without, and nor did she want to.

Grady knew Ashley was watching him. Not that he minded, he watched her far more than he would ever reveal to anyone. As she fed her rumbling stomach, her little moans of enjoyment made his body ache to have her again.

She had been a maid, an innocent debutante, he ought to offer marriage, and he would. He would go to the duke tomorrow and ask for her hand, although he did not know what kind of reception he would receive from the gentleman.

They had not spoken in years, Derby's father when he was alive believing the falsehoods his sire had put about town, and he couldn't help but wonder if the duke would too think as his father had.

Many in London did. Too many to count.

"You look very serious all of a sudden. Is something wrong?" she asked him, touching his arm.

He shook his head, covering her hand with his. "Nothing is wrong," he said, leaning back onto the many cushions surrounding them. "Tell me, are you enjoying yourself? Have you ever had a water picnic before on a Venetian boat in London? I hope you have not."

"Of course, I had one just last week with my other lover," she teased, joining him on the cushions.

Grady grabbed her and tickled her until she begged for release. "Tell me that is not true," he said, making her pay for such teasing, even though he knew she did not mean a word of it.

She laughed, the sound infectious and making him smile. Never in all the years he'd lived in London had he ever laughed and smiled as much as he had these past weeks with Ashley.

"I promise, it is only you. Only ever will be you," she admitted.

He met her gaze and could see the truth of her words in her dark-brown eyes that promised years of happiness, of contentment. Nothing like he had ever known. Not even running the gaming hell brought him as much pleasure as being with Ashley did.

"I know exactly how you mean," he replied, wanting her to know that even if he had not spoken the words to ask for her hand, he would soon have the right. After tomorrow when he visited the duke, they would be betrothed, and nothing would ever come between them.

He would tell her of the rumors and his father's cruelty once they were married. She did not need to worry unnecessarily until after the nuptials. Not that she had anything to worry about.

Grady closed the space between them and took her lips in a searing kiss. She met him halfway, her arms going about his neck, pulling him atop her.

He did not deny her. He wanted her. His body burned with the need to be with her again. Under the canopy, they could not be seen by the oarsman, and Grady saw no reason to deny them both the other.

"This may be a little difficult with your breeches," he whispered.

"Hurry," she gasped, undulating against his hard cock.

He groaned, flipped her onto her stomach, and pulled her back against him.

She looked over her shoulder, her hair pooling down her back. Damn, she was beautiful, a siren tempting him to his watery grave. "What are you doing?" she asked, her eyes burning with interest.

"Do you trust me?" he questioned, reaching about her falls and ripping them open before slipping her breeches down her ass.

He took the opportunity to squeeze her pert globes, kissing both of them for good measure.

She gasped and groaned when he kissed the base of her spine.

"I trust you," she breathed.

Grady kneeled behind her, having never ripped at his falls so fast in his life. His cock sprang free into his hand, and he came over her, guiding himself into her hot, tight cunny.

Bloody hell, she felt good, tight and wet, her juicy cunny telling him more than words ever could how she needed him as much as he needed her. She moaned his name into the cushions, egging him on.

It was madness, of course. Perhaps they could be seen from the shore or other passing boats, but he did not care. All he wanted was to fuck her, take her, make her come, and draw his own release forth while doing so.

She came up onto her hands and pushed against him as he took her with relentless strokes. The sweet sounds of her enjoyment were music to his ears.

His balls tightened, and he knew he would not last long. Grady reached around her hips, teasing the little bead that begged for attention.

"Grady," she moaned. "Touch me. Take me," she said, thrusting herself harder against him.

He continued his steady pace, his cock working her as his hand teased. She rocked onto him, and he could feel the first tremors of her release contract about his cock.

She screamed his name, heedless of where they were or who operated the boat mere inches from them.

Grady let her ride her release through before he came hard, pumped his seed deep into her cunny, and reveled in the feel of her taking him, giving him as much as he gave her.

He leaned down and kissed her back before slipping free. He pulled her beside him on the cushions, her breeches still down about her knees. He had never seen a more erotic sight in his life.

She reached up and clasped his cheek. "I adore you," she said, her visage one of contentment.

He kissed her softly. "I adore you too," he said, and for the first time, the adoration may be so much more than that mediocre word.

Love reverberated about in his mind, but there was time to declare such sentiments. From tomorrow he would tell her. Tell her that he loved her. Give her the opportunity to choose him. Let her decide if marrying Grady Kolten, gaming hell owner and social outcast, was suitable for her future.

Damn it all to hell, he hoped it was.

# TWENTY-ONE

G rady was escorted into the Duke of Derby's large library on Berkeley Square the following afternoon. He pushed down the nerves that balled in his gut. There was no reason for him to be concerned. The duke was, from all accounts, a reasonable man and not the type to believe rumors that could not be substantiated, especially if those rumors were untrue.

Still, so much rode on the duke's decision today. He needed to marry Ashley. That was one certainty he knew more than any other. Living without her, knowing she existed somewhere else or belonged to another was a torture he could not endure. Not ever.

The duke had to say yes to his request, which was all there was about it.

The butler announced his arrival, and the duke stood, gesturing for him to sit. Grady did as instructed and did not miss that the duke did not wish him any greeting upon his entry.

"Your Grace," Grady said, breaking the silence. "Good to see you again."

The duke sat, watching him keenly. "Lord Howley, it has been a long time."

"It has," he agreed. "Congratulations on your marriage. I have not seen you since you became a husband."

A small smile lifted the duke's lips. Clearly, the rumors were true, and the duke's marriage was a love match. Much like Grady was certain he had with Ashley. If he could gain the approval to go ahead with marrying her.

"Thank you. I'm very content," he answered. "You wished an audience with me today, but I must confess that I'm confused as to why."

Grady nodded, all understandable. "I came here because there is a certain matter that I wish to discuss with you."

"Really?" the duke asked, lifting one brow in disbelief. "I find that hard to believe. You are Grady Kolten, the Earl of Howley who runs a scandalous gaming hell in the East End, are you not? From what I have heard, you never need anyone's help or good opinions, and certainly, I do not darken your door, so today's visit is a mystery to me."

Grady ignored what he felt was a small barb marked against him and remembered why he was here. To secure the approval to ask for Ashley's hand. He and the duke did not need to be friends. He merely needed him to agree to his request.

"That is true when it comes to the business, of course, but I'm not here because of my hell. I'm here because I wish to ask for Miss Ashley Woodville's hand in marriage and would like your consent before I do so. I know that she regards you and her family highly and would not want to do anything to cause others pain."

"What?" the duke barked, clearly surprised. "You're asking for Ashley's hand? However do you know the girl?"

he asked, his brow coming together in a severe frown. "Or do I not want to know how it is that you're acquainted with my wife's sister."

"I attended her coming-out ball and another in the Season. We get along well and enjoy each other's company. I think if you ask Miss Woodville, she will disclose she agrees with my request. It is something that we both wish for."

"The hell you are," the duke snapped. "You run one of London's seediest, most unethical gaming hells in London, and you expect me to allow my ward, a young woman my parents-in-law placed into my care for the Season, to marry a blackguard like yourself." The duke leaned back in his chair, clearly affronted. "And that isn't even taking your father's claims of illegitimacy."

Grady took a calming breath, having expected a little push back on his request to marry the duke's sister-in-law, but not this vehement denial he was receiving.

"My father is a bastard. I would have thought, having had a father yourself who was cut from the same cloth, you would have looked upon me more favorably than that."

The duke gaped before he thought better of whatever he was about to say. He held up his hands, trying to calm the situation that Grady could feel was escalating to a point that neither gentleman wished to face.

"You are right, my father was the worst of men, and from what I know of yours, he is not much better. But your mother fled London years ago, and there is a saying, is there not? The innocent remain and the guilty flee. True or not," the duke continued, "there is a cloud of uncertainly to your name, and that shadow will darken any woman you choose to be your wife."

Grady shook his head. He was legitimate. His mama, a

woman he believed and trusted with his life, was already three months pregnant when she was raped. His father was an ass and one who did not understand the workings of a woman's body.

A stupid, naïve prick.

"My mother did nothing wrong, and I'll not have her name dragged into any slanderous lies my father or anyone else dredges up. I'm legitimate, and I will be the Duke of Blackhaven when my father is dead, and nothing, not rumors or untruths anyone spreads about me, will change that fact."

"Does Ashley know of this past scandal?" Derby asked him.

Grady swallowed, knowing that she did not. He shook his head, shamed that he had not told her everything about himself when he had the chance. He should have told her before this meeting with her family. If they were to ask her opinion on his past, it would shock her and possibly make her hesitate. Never a good outcome when he hoped to gain her support for their wishes.

"No, she does not know."

"Then I suggest you tell her, here and now, and we shall see what she wants to do, but I must warn you, Howley, I do not think this is a good suit for her."

"And why is that, because Lord Walsh and others of his ilk are sniffing about her skirts? The man is a cad. If you think I'm a wastrel, you have seen nothing compared to the antics of that man."

The duke narrowed his eyes, thinking over his words. "I have not heard anything untoward against Lord Walsh. In fact, he has acted the gentleman most of all the men courting Ashley. I would not be against a match with the appropriate earl." The duke stood and walked to the mantel, ringing the bell.

"If you saw him in my club and others, you would not be of that opinion," Grady interjected just as the butler entered, and Derby summoned Ashley and her sister, the duchess, to join them.

Grady knew the moment she entered the room, the scent of jasmine kissed his senses, and he breathed deep, turning to smile at her. She grinned back. A light, rosy blush appeared on her cheeks.

She was so pure and fetching, and he wanted her for himself.

He bowed to the duchess. "Good afternoon, Your Grace, Miss Woodville," he said, waiting for them to sit on two chairs the duke had positioned for them.

Grady sat and hoped he was not wrong about Ashley. That she would see past the lies she was about to be told and stand by him anyway because she loved him.

Just as he knew to the very depth of his heart that he loved her too.

A shley adjusted her gown, laughing to herself that this had been the first time in quite some time since Grady had seen her dressed not as a man.

She looked between Derby and Grady and couldn't help but notice the tension that seemed to radiate within the room. What was going on? Why was Grady here, and why did the duke look like he was ready to commit murder?

His thunderous visage did not bode well for any of them.

The terrible thought that someone had seen them and told the duke of their outings made her want to cast up her accounts. Had the dreadful Lord Walsh followed through on his threat?

She clasped her hands in her lap, hoping her face did not reveal the tumultuous thoughts in her mind.

"Ashley, my dear, Lord Howley has come here today to request my approval for your hand in marriage. If you're willing, of course—"

"Yes," she said, jumping up and going to Grady, pulling him to stand. "I will marry you," she said, elation thrumming through her like a drug. She wanted to jump for joy and hug him but thought better of it because of the company they kept.

"Ah, before we get to that," the duke said, pulling her from Grady and sitting her back beside her sister. "There are some matters to discuss."

Grady threw her a small smile, and she could feel heat burning her cheeks at the public display of, well...desperation she had just shown them all. Not that she was overly desperate, but she wanted to marry Grady so much that the knowledge he was here and trying to gain her hand had left her giddy with excitement.

"What matters?" the duchess asked, taking Ashley's hand as if she foresaw something Ashley did not.

"Howley, would you care to tell Ashley of your family and the scandal that follows you that will pursue Ashley should she agree to be your wife?"

Grady glared at the duke but turned to her, and she could see that he was steeling himself to explain something she did not know. Whatever it was troubled him and made her heart race and her stomach churn.

What was he going to say, and why did she feel that it would not be good? Not good at all.

# TWENTY-TWO

Grady met her eye, and Ashley could see the concern burning within his. "Miss Woodville, before any consents are given or promises made and contracts signed, there are some things you need to know of me."

Ashley fiddled with her sister's hand, not liking how Grady was talking or the tone that seemed off and careful. Nothing like the usual sweet, amusing tone he often took with her.

He continued, "You know of the gaming hell that I own. And that my mother has little to do with society, but there is a reason for that, which you need to be aware of before any more on the matter of marriage is discussed."

Ashley glanced at Derby and noted his concern. She took a calming breath, hoping whatever she was about to hear was not too shocking. The thought of not being married to Grady was a situation she could not abide. She wanted him with every part that made her whole. She could not live with a little of herself missing.

"Please go on and tell me. I'm certain everyone is

making a bigger deal of whatever it is than is needed," she said, chuckling to try to break the tension in the room. It did not work. Oh dear, this meeting was not proceeding as she had hoped when first entering the room and seeing Grady with the duke.

"I am estranged from my father. You have seen that yourself, but what you do not know is that he banished my mother from London and me for many years due to his belief that I'm illegitimate."

Ashley felt her mouth gape at the declaration and shut it with a snap. "You're not legitimate? But that cannot be right. You're an earl and future duke. How can your father believe you're not legitimate and still have you as his heir?"

Grady frowned, clearly searching for the right words to explain this to her. "My mother was accused of having an affair many years ago, and my father believed that I'm the product of that union. I am not, and I believe my mother when she told me she was pregnant long before the breach in her marriage occurred. I will not go into particulars, but my father cannot prove that I'm not his, and therefore the Blackhaven ducal estate and the honorary title of earl that I now carry is mine to inherit. I will inherit it, and I will not allow any scandal to blacken your name should you agree to marry me."

Ashley sat stupefied for a moment, having not expected such a scandalous affair to be the reason behind why Grady was estranged from his father.

Was it true? She would have to take Grady's word for it, and his mother, whom she did not know. But she had not met her before, and she did indeed live outside of London. Had she birthed a son to a man who was not her husband?

And could Ashley marry such a man?

Place her heart and future happiness into his hands and

hope that such a historic scandal would not tarnish her and their children?

"I need you to believe me, Ashley. No matter what you're debating in your mind right now, I am my father's son, no matter what he says. He is a pigheaded fool who can never listen to reason, and he lost his family for such foolishness. Do not make the same mistake and lose a man who sits before you this very day offering marriage to a lie. A man who loves you so very much that the thought of losing you makes me sick to my soul."

Ashley bit her lip, having never heard him say such wonderful things before. But could she marry him, never knowing if what he said was the truth or not?

She wanted to tell him she loved him too, but the words would not come. She needed time to think, to decide. To marry Grady could mean scandal, affecting her younger sister's chances next year during her coming out. Not to mention her sisters were already part of the *ton*. She did not want them shamed by their association with her and Grady.

Whatever would she do?

"I need time," she managed to mumble.

The door burst open at that moment, and Lord Walsh walked in, his face flushed and his cravat and coat ruffled. The butler stumbled in after him, his clothing worse for wear.

Had they been fighting in the foyer?

The duke stood, a thunderous glare on his visage that Ashley had never seen before. "What is the meaning of this? Lord Walsh, this is a private conversation that I do not remember inviting you to. Leave. Now, before I ruffle more than your cravat as my butler did," he stated, clearly sensing they had been in fisticuffs in the foyer, his words brooking no argument.

Lord Walsh sniffed as if the duke had not said a word and merely sauntered closer to the desk, pointing a short, stumpy finger at Grady. "You cannot under any circumstances be considering this man's suit toward Miss Woodville," Lord Walsh said to the duke. "There are things about him, about them both, that should rule him out immediately, and I'm here to save her reputation from the blackguard who professes anything that he has been sitting here declaring."

Grady cast a concerned glance at Ashley, and she cringed, knowing only too well what Lord Walsh was referring to.

"What do you mean?" the duchess asked, pinning Lord Walsh with a scowl equal to her husband's. "You sound like you're accusing them of untoward behavior."

Lord Walsh nodded solemnly. "That is true, Your Grace. That is the very nature of my visiting with you today. I heard that Lord Howley had called upon you, and I knew what he was about and his intentions here."

"And your intentions?" the duke asked. "Will we learn of them at any point today, or will you merely insinuate knowing something while telling us nothing?"

Lord Walsh smirked, licking his lips when he met Ashley's eye. A cold, detestable shiver ran down her spine, and never in her life had she loathed someone as much as she hated the man before her.

"This man who proclaims to be a gentleman, an earl, and future duke mind you, has been escorting your charge about London in the dead of night. Attending *demimonde* balls and parties. Rides in the park, unchaperoned escorts to orphanages, his gaming hell, Whites, and even a workhouse."

The duchess gasped at the mention of the last location, and Ashley shook her head. "We have not visited a workhouse. Not yet, at least," she added, grinding her teeth at the man's audacity and his threats.

"Where you have visited is bad enough should the *ton* learn of your nightly excursions," Lord Walsh quipped. "I am here to save Miss Woodville, of course. Something that Lord Howley was hell-bent on doing the opposite of. I shall marry her, and the truth will die with a vow before a priest."

Ashley scoffed. The duke looked between her and Grady. "Is what he says true? Have you been sneaking out and visiting such locales around London with Lord Howley?"

The heat of shame kissed her cheeks, and she bit her lip, hating that she had played hazard with her reputation. That she had lied to her sister and brother-in-law, two people she respected and loved. "It is true, and I'm sorry for my actions, but they have come to an end. Lord Walsh threatened me with his knowledge of my excursions and demanded I marry him. His lordship coming here this afternoon is merely his attempt yet again to gain his way."

"Without my way, my dear, you will have no future."

"She could have a future with me," Grady stated, holding her gaze. "Whether she is ruined or not by your loose mouth. I shall not ever let her feel less than who she is."

"Nor I, except with my proposal, she keeps her reputation and status in the *ton*," Lord Walsh stated.

Ashley could not look away from Grady. He truly did love her. But what was she to do?

One thing she knew for certain, she would not marry Lord Walsh.

"Only over my dead body will you touch a single hair on Miss Woodville's head. You're a cad, a debaucher and I have little doubt, one tup away from catching the pox. You chastise Miss Woodville for her learnings, and yet you do far worse in the world every night. The apple does not fall far from the tree when it comes to a Walsh and his father's reputation," Grady stated, his tone deadly.

Ashley did not know what he meant, but the meaning had clearly hit a nerve if the paling of Lord Walsh's face from the implication of Grady's words was anything to go by.

"Ashley will not be happy with Walsh, and you would be foolish to force that union on her simply because you, like so many others, believe me to be illegitimate. I am not, and I will be a duke one day, and when that day comes, you will rue this day should you allow Ashley to marry a man, any man, who does not love her as I do."

"The choice is Ashley's," the duke returned. "I would not force her, but there is more than your feelings for her at stake. Her family, her unwed sister, and how she would be received in society. And if Lord Walsh follows through on his threats, honest or not, she is ruined, which will impact all of us."

The room spun, and Ashley's stomach whirled. She stood and fled. Ran upstairs, anywhere than before the four ridiculing, judging eyes upon her. Anywhere but that damn library where she could not think and decide.

What she would do for the rest of her life.

# TWENTY-THREE

Ashley sat in the window seat in her room, staring out over the ducal grounds that were as immaculate as they were grand. A light knock sounded on the door, and she called to enter, turning to see Hailey slip into her chamber.

"Ashley, are you well? You looked so pale when you left, and well, we really must talk, dearest," she said, sitting beside her.

She sighed, unsure how or what else there was to say. "If I do not marry Lord Walsh, I'm ruined. If I marry Lord Howley, I'm ruined. If I marry neither, I'm ruined. What else is there to say?" Ashley wiped angrily at a wayward tear that dared slip down her cheeks. What a mess the whole situation was. Not to mention at this very moment, she could not think of one thing that could help her decide what to do.

"The situation is very grave, but I cannot understand why it is that you acted as you have. Are you not happy here? Have we not kept you entertained? I thought you were welcoming the Season and all its diversions?" Hailey asked her.

Ashley grabbed her hand, squeezing it, not ever wanting her sister to think she was ungrateful or unhappy, for she had not been. Never once since she had traveled to London. "You and Derby have been so wonderful to me, and I am happy with the Season. I have met friends and had adventures, but the moment I met Lord Howley, I felt something that I had never felt before and knew I had to engage him somehow in helping me merely so I could be near him. I did not think Lord Walsh would see me on my outings, but he did, and now he's trying to use that knowledge to his advantage."

"As the duke has stated to Lord Walsh after you left, our word is against his as there has been no other mention or rumors of your escapades. I'm sure we can deal with Lord Walsh well enough, but Lord Howley is another matter."

"What are you saying?" Ashley asked, the glimmer of hope she had dissipating at her sister's words.

"Lord Howley, illegitimate or not, runs one of London's most exclusive and scandalous gaming hells. With or without his father's title and money, he could keep you safe and living a luxurious life. But there have been things said after his sporadic appearances at the *ton* events this Season. I have not shared them with you, for I did not think they were relevant to you and your life." Her sister threw her a consoling look. "Lord Howley is tolerated in society and nothing more."

Ashley frowned, hating the idea of anyone tolerating Grady. He deserved so much more than that.

"More than likely because so many gentlemen of the *ton* owe him large sums of money and would not dare kick him out of their events. But there would be slights and exclusions against you because of that should you marry him. And that would mean the Season you have enjoyed so much could become so different from the one you have relished this year. It could affect how much we see you here in London during those months. It could impact who looks to Millie next year. There is much you must think upon and decide what it is you're willing to risk to have him."

Ashley jumped as thunder rumbled over the city, the windowpane rattling at its intensity. Dark storm clouds threatened the afternoon sky, parallel to the emotions rioting within her.

"I do not know what to do," she admitted, the tears she had been holding back released like a flood. "If I do not marry him, I do not think I could marry anyone. I love him as he loves me, but I know that love comes at a cost."

"Do you love him, though, Ashley? He did not tell you the rumor he may be illegitimate before today. That his mother had been sent to live in the country because the duke believed her to be a light skirt who birthed a child who was not the rightful heir? Has he told you of his past, of his future, or has he merely seduced you into loving him without giving you the truth so you may know who you are actually in love with?"

Ashley gaped, having never thought of her time with Grady like that. In truth, she knew very little of him at all. Had he kept things from her so she would fall in love, and their parting would be almost impossible for her to do?

If there was no truth to the accusations laid against him, why did he not tell her himself what some of the *ton* believed? What his father believed?

"I love him, I do. But there are so many things to consider, not only my happiness," she said, meeting her sister's soothing eyes. "I'm sorry for not acting as expected."

Hailey smiled, pulling her into a comforting hug. "We are not always, not any of us, perfect. Do not think that I am, for I am not, but we will get through this, no matter your choice."

She nodded, her mind scrambling to decide what she would choose. Her family, her love, or her reputation...

G rady watched Ashley flee from the room. He wanted to pummel Lord Walsh, who pretended he was alarmed and upset by Ashley's sudden departure. The man was not fooling anyone. He did not have a bone in his body capable of any real affection. Not for anyone other than himself.

"Look what your influence has done to Miss Woodville. Now she is upset," Walsh stated, gesturing to the door and glaring at Grady.

"It is unlikely that Ashley will consent to be your wife, Walsh. During this Season, not at any time has she hinted at a growing affection toward your lordship. Even after you have been more than obvious with yours," the duke added.

"Well." Walsh blushed. "That is because she is confused at present. But let me remind you, Derby, I have friends, rapscallions they may be, but they would be willing to ruin her should I wish it so. And should she deny me, I will wish it so, do you understand?"

Grady stood, coming to stand and tower over the dandy. "You forget that I, along with the duke, also have friends in powerful places. You may have tried to tarnish me in front of Ashley today, but it will not work. She will see through your lies."

"I will ruin her should I not get my way," Walsh smirked. "What a shame, but then a fitting wife for a man who is the same. A pariah in society, a by-blow, a—"

The crack of Grady's punch to Walsh's nose was music to his ears. He watched him with satisfaction as the man flew backward and landed with a thump on the thick Aubusson rug at their feet.

The duke stood, leaning over his desk to stare annoyingly at the unconscious man.

"He will be even more vicious toward you and Ashley should she forgo the risks and marries you anyway."

Grady shrugged. "I think it is unlikely she would choose me over her family. They are close from what I could gather, and she would not do anything to jeopardize her younger sister's chances next year."

The duke nodded, and for the first time that day, Grady saw a flicker of concern on His Grace's visage. Did he worry that Ashley would never be happy by not marrying him? That she would one day realize she had picked the wrong alternative?

"I'm sorry for all of this, Howley. If you are legitimate, then there are no words for how sorry I am that you've been tarnished all these years. I know what it is like to have a cruel father and a mother who paid the price for that cruelty." The duke sighed, striding to the window, glancing back as Lord Walsh groaned on the floor and then stilled once again. "If it were only that, we could somehow prove you were legitimate, that would be one thing, but your reputation is atrocious. The stories I have heard of your time at the gaming hell and the antics that go on there, I cannot allow Ashley to enter that world."

Grady could understand. He would not allow his sister or daughter, should he have one, to enter a union of that kind that would push her toward such a life. But nor could he see himself with anyone but Ashley. She was his sunshine in a cold, gray London.

What would he do without her?

"And Walsh? What of him?" Grady asked, kicking the man's boot and gaining another moan of protest.

"We can ignore his knowledge of Ashley's mistakes and term them as a sad attempt from a man determined to marry her and not willing to allow her to marry anyone else. Her friends will vouch for her whereabouts, and there is no proof. No one else saw Ashley galivanting about London in men's clothing. Walsh," the duke said, his lip lifting in distaste, "will slink back to the hellish hole he came from and stay there for all I care."

The thought gave Grady some comfort. At least Ashley would not be forced into a union she did not want. She may not be able to have him, but nor would she have to endure Walsh.

A small consolation that he would have to be content with. "I will take my leave. Have word sent to me at the hell when Ashley has made her choice."

The duke nodded. "Of course."

Grady strode from the room, resisting the urge to glance up to the first floor. *Please choose me*, he silently prayed. *Pick me and be happy.* That was all he wanted and what he hoped Ashley did too.

# TWENTY-FOUR

Ashley did not remain in London. The endless balls and parties lost their luster since her departure from Grady. She had not seen or heard from him for a week. The separation ate at her sanity, and she knew she had to leave to return home and see her mama and papa, and her best friend Daphne in Grafton.

Her friend Daphne sat on a chair in her mother's downstairs drawing room before the fire, their catch-up long overdue. Ashley had relayed to her friend all that had happened in London. Her nights out with her friends. How she had met Lord Howley through a dare. How much she had enjoyed his company and banter, not to mention his kisses.

"And this Lord Walsh has followed through on his threat and spread the rumor of you dressing up in men's clothing and galivanting about London with Lord Howley. What does the *ton* believe, do you know?" Daphne asked.

Thankfully the *ton* had more sense than Lord Walsh had given them credit for. "They do not believe him. His accusations have been met with confusion and disbelief."

141

True to the duke's word, he had made Lord Walsh seem like a jealous cur who could not get his way and therefore made up fanciful tattletales about Miss Woodville in an attempt to tarnish her name and gain a wife.

"In any case, I received a letter from Hailey only yesterday, and she mentioned that Lord Walsh and his good friend Lord Fenton had fled England for France. Let us hope that is where they will stay," she said.

Daphne reached out, squeezing her hand. "Well, you're miserable here. I can see it written on your pretty features, and I will no longer stand for it. You must return to London and fight for what you want," Daphne stated heatedly, pointing her finger at Ashley for good measure.

"Grady has not written to me nor begged for my return. The day he told me the truth, my actions made it appear that I believed what his mother was accused of. I hesitated in my choice even after he vehemently denied being a by-blow, and I think it has impacted my chances of happiness." Maybe he was angry with her? Did he think she thought his mother was unfaithful and he was the result of that union? The more she thought on the matter, the more she understood that he could never believe such a thing.

"He said to the duke that he would wait for your reply. Maybe you ought to write to him and tell him you think you made a mistake." The sound of a carriage on the drive caught their attention. Daphne frowned and stood, walking to the window to investigate.

"Someone is here. A woman, by the looks of it. She's very regal, and gah, has the loveliest hair for a woman of her age."

Ashley quickly joined Daphne and gasped. The woman was the spitting image of Grady. Was it his mother? Had his mother traveled to Grafton to speak to her or her parents?

Maybe she wanted to chastise Ashley on her antics. Of making trouble for her son that he did not need.

Ashley swallowed her fear and turned as the door opened and a footman announced the Duchess of Blackhaven to see her.

Daphne's eyes were as wide as saucers, and Ashley knew hers were a mirror image. They both dipped into curtsies before, without warning, Daphne fled the room, closing the door with a decided snap on her chance of escape.

Some friend she was. Ashley would have a word or two about her friend's hasty departure.

"Miss Ashley Woodville, I presume," the duchess said not unkindly, her voice soft but with an edge of steel. "I have been longing to meet you for quite some time. Grady has told me a lot about you."

Ashley gestured for Her Grace to sit. Her mind spun at the thought of Grady talking to anyone about her. But then, the woman before her was his mama, his closest ally and friend. Of course he would tell her of his troubles. And how much trouble Ashley had been to him.

"It is an honor to meet you, Your Grace," she said. "I hope you have left Lord Howley in good health back in London." She was so pitiful asking after him in such a roundabout way, but she was desperate to know if he was as miserable as she was. If he longed for her as much as she yearned for him.

"He is well, Miss Woodville. As well as can be expected when his heart is broken," she said, the small, sad smile making Ashley's heart pinch.

Ashley glanced down at her hands, working them in her lap. Anything but stare at the woman before her who did nothing but dredge up a pang of guilt after she returned home.

"I'm sorry for that. Truly I am. But I was so shaken by what I learned from Lord Howley that day that I did not know what to do. Of what society thinks of him and, in turn, myself should I marry his lordship that I panicked. I returned home because I needed to see my friend and be with my parents. To decide what is best for my family in this circumstance."

"And that is why I'm here, to help explain." The duchess frowned as if the memory she was about to relay was too painful to recall. "My son does not trust many in the world other than myself, and that is partly my fault. I was so angry for so long that he associated that anger through me as seeing everyone as enemies, people to be untrustworthy or harmful to us until they proved otherwise. And while that trait has assisted him with his business and been a worthy ally, it has also had its downfalls. But with you, Miss Woodville, for the first time in my son's life, I see that he trusted you, loves you, and I think you need to give him another chance to prove he's worthy of your love in return."

The knowledge that Grady's mama even believed him to be in love with her was music to her ears. She had not been sure he would be after their altercation. She wanted nothing more than to go to him. To apologize, to tell him that she loved him too and that she did not care if they were both pariahs of society, so long as they had each other.

The thought of not living by society's rules had its positives that she had come to face these past days, and most of them would make life interesting and much more exciting than anything she had envisioned for herself before.

"Will you tell me why he could not share the truth of his past? I'm trying to understand it all, but it makes so little sense."

The duchess stared toward the fire, watching the

hungry flames consume the wood. "I married the Duke of Blackhaven because I loved him. We were made for each other, and life was perfect when I conceived our son. I waited to tell the duke. I wanted to be sure and not disappoint him as I knew he wanted children, but during my second month, almost three, I attended a rout, a night like any other, I thought, but I was wrong. A man attended, one of the peerage whom I had denied my hand when he had asked a year before I married the duke. I thought us acquaintances, congenial but not close. Pregnant as I was, I frequented the retiring room more often than most ladies, and during one of my sojourns upstairs, this man accosted me."

Ashley felt the blood drain from her face at the duchess's words, and a sinking feeling pooled in her belly that she was not going to like this story at all. That this was not what she had thought was the reason behind the rumors of Grady's illegitimacy.

The duchess played with her hands in her lap, rolling the wedding ring that she still wore in circular motions. "He pushed me into a room, threatened to punch me should I not remain quiet and do as he said. I was pregnant, and somehow he had known to threaten me in a way that would equate to my immediate compliance. I did not want my child harmed, so I did not make a sound. I lay there and let him do his business. I was so ashamed," the duchess said, her voice breaking.

Ashley went to her, taking her hands and holding them tight. "You have nothing to be ashamed for. He was the villain in this, not you. You did nothing wrong."

The duchess cleared her throat, her focus on that long-ago time that so obviously still caused her pain. "The man crowed to my husband about having me.

How I had laid down like a doxy and accepted him with open arms. All lies, of course, but my husband, a man who loved me, became so consumed with hurt and anger that he directed that emotion toward me instead of the real culprit. When I told him I was expecting, he did not believe it was his and cast me out to the dowager house. I have lived there ever since. That is where Grady was raised before he moved to London."

"But would you not have had Grady three months earlier than the duke expected if he believed such a tale? Did he not, even then, start to think that maybe he was wrong to accuse you of adultery?"

"He was so angry that he would not see reason. He merely believed that I was having an affair before that night, but Grady resembles Blackhaven as much as he resembles me, and I know the truth, even if the duke is too pigheaded to believe it."

"I'm so sorry, Your Grace. How you must have suffered. That should never have happened to you." Ashley swallowed the lump in her throat, hating the idea of such a vile act being done upon anyone. How dare the gentleman violate another human being and gloat over the fact afterward. What a horrible man.

"Which is why I also caution you toward Lord Walsh and explain why my son dislikes him so. It was Lord Walsh's father, the Marquess of Gibson, who assaulted me that night and took liberties that were not his to have. His son is cut from the same cloth, and Grady does not want to see you or anyone aligned with him. The family is not what they portray."

Bile rose in her throat, and deep down inside her, she knew what the duchess was saying was true. To think at the beginning of the Season she liked Lord Walsh. What had she been thinking?

"That is shocking indeed," she managed, thinking about what she had learned and what it meant for Grady and her. She had made such a mistake believing there may be any truth to the claim against him. How she wished she could take so many things back.

"Why did Grady not tell me this himself? Had I known, I would never have acted as I did. I would never have left him alone. Does he think I believe the lies? I do not, I assure you. Being home, I've come to realize that I never did."

The duchess threw her a small smile. "Grady would not tell anyone what happened to me. It is my story to tell, and I had hoped he had moved on from what happened to me, but it seems the rumors are still circulating. I'm going to put a stop to them. I will reenter society and stare down anyone who tries to slander my name. It is time that Lord Walsh and his father the Marquess of Gibson were treated as the pests that they are and be shunned instead."

"And the duke?" Ashley asked. "Your husband?"

"Well, he will have to learn to live with his wife again. Over the many years I've lived alone, I've become quite strong of mind and opinionated. I think it is time he heard what I have to say for both the past and future. My son deserves his place in society, and for too long, I have let him live in the shadows in East London. But not anymore. He is a future duke, and he will start acting like one, or he too will have my opinions on the matter known."

Ashley smiled, feeling lightness and excitement for what was to come for the first time in days. Her future with Grady, if he could forgive her for being naïve and stupid.

"May I ask something of you, Your Grace?" she asked.

The duchess nodded. "Anything, my dear."

"Will you allow me to ride back with you to London? I need to return and see Grady. Try and make things right."

She smiled, and the gesture made a lump form in her throat. Grady looked so similar to his mama, which made her miss him all the more. "Allow you to ride back with me? I would have demanded that you do. I want my son to be happy, and I believe you, my dear, are the only one who will make it so."

He was the only one who would make her happy also.

CHAPTER

# TWENTY-FIVE

Nerves pooled in Ashley's stomach as she paced the inside of Grady's office at his gaming hell. She was not dressed as a man today, deciding that if she wanted to marry him, people would have to start getting used to seeing her with him as she was.

A woman of the *ton*, of family and fortune. That was if he would take her back. She prayed that he would forgive her, that he still loved her as much as she loved him.

He had looked so disappointed when she had seen him last. As if she had proved herself like so many others in the *ton*, believing vicious, disgusting lies about his mother and, in turn, himself.

The door flew open, and she jumped. Grady strode into the room and came to an abrupt halt at the sight of her. His eyes were bloodshot and dark circles sat beneath them as if he had not slept in days.

His clothing was immaculate as usual, but there was a dishevelment about him she had not seen before. A part of her broke at the thought of him having just returned after a night with another woman. Had he been with someone else? Was he so angry with her that he had forgotten her already? Had he seen her as unworthy?

"Why are you here? Should you not be with Lord Walsh, eating up his lies about my mother and me? I did not think a lady would want to be seen associating with the bastard Earl of Howley."

Ashley cringed. He had become angry since she had left, and she could not blame him. She had fled London and with no promise of returning. Had she been in his shoes, she would have been of similar disposition.

"You're not a bastard, and I'm sorry you think that I thought that, but I was merely shocked by what I heard. Deep down, I never believed it, and when your mother came to see me and explained everything to me, I knew what I felt the first time hearing the tale to be true. That you're legitimate. That you're wonderful and loving and funny and everything that is good in my life. I know we met under strange circumstances, and I was a pest, but I love you, Grady Kolten, Earl of Howley, future Duke of Blackhaven, and I want you to be my husband. I want to marry you and bedamned what anyone else thinks or says on the matter." Ashley shrugged. "I do not care so long as I have you." There, she had said it. All that she had come here to say. Grady would either forgive her, or he would not. But at least she had tried, and that was all that she could do.

Grady stared at Ashley. Had the chit gone mad? When he had seen her last, she had been confused, that he was certain, but she should have believed him. She knew him better than most, and it should have been enough for her that he defended his mother's honor, and she believed that and nothing else.

But she had not.

"I know I never told you about my mother because it should have been enough at my word that when I said a wrong was done to her during her marriage that you ought to have believed me."

Ashley walked past him and panic assailed him that she was leaving. He rounded on her to stop her and felt like a complete idiot when she merely closed the door.

"I should have believed you," she said. "But everyone was coming at me. Derby with his warning of the hell being bad for my sister Millie's chances of marriage. Lord Walsh was throwing out that you're illegitimate and that he would out us for our scandalous behavior. I was scared, unsure, and terrified someone would make me marry Lord Walsh, a horrendous outcome to even think of. I was scared that I would lose you, and I would have to make my family suffer to marry you, so I fled."

"You ought to have stayed," he chastised.

"And you ought to have told me the truth. Had you done so, I would not have questioned if you respected and loved me as you said you did. Are there no lies between two people who profess such emotions? You ought to have trusted me with that secret. No matter how grievous. I know you were protecting your mama, and it does you credit that you were, but if I'm to be your wife, you should have told me."

"So I'm to blame now, is that it?" he asked, hating that he was being obtuse. Pigheaded simply because he was mad at her and himself for not being as honest as he should have.

She glared up at him, and his heart did a little flip that she was indeed back in his office, back within arm's reach. God damn, he'd missed his sunshine.

"We agree then that we've both acted wrong?" he said, clasping her hips and pulling her close. He'd missed her since she had left London, and for a time, he had wondered if she would ever return.

"If we're to move forward, I think we must agree to that statement." She wrapped her arms around his waist, staring up at him. "I'm sorry, Grady. Since being back in London, my sister has pointed out that your father—and your mama is right—and you do look alike. But your smile and kind eyes are all your mama's doing. Seeing her at Grafton made me miss you more than I thought I ever could, but she is not the reason I'm here."

"She isn't?" he asked, pushing a lock of hair from her face so he could see her better.

"I was going to return to London to be with you no matter your past. When I was away from you, I realized that I did not care if you were legitimate or not. No other man will do for me. You've ruined me for anyone else, and there is only you."

A weight lifted from his chest, and for the first time in what seemed forever, he could breathe again. He wrapped her in his arms, holding her close. "I would give this up if it meant that I could win you. While you were away, I thought of nothing but how to get you back. The thought of you marrying someone other than me drove me to the brink of murder, namely Walsh, for I thought you might be forced into a union with him. I could not endure such torture to be separated from you. Not ever again."

Ashley swiped at a tear, huddling against him tighter. "I could not bear the thought of marrying anyone else either. And do not concern yourself with Lord Walsh. Derby has put paid to his threats, and I believe his lordship and his friend have fled to France. I should think they will not darken our doorsteps for a very long time."

"But by marrying me, what of your family? Your sister Millie?" he asked. "What if our marriage impacts her chances of a good match?"

"It will not," Ashley assured him. "My sisters are high enough in the peerage to cut anyone out of society who would say anything against Millie. And for all your wild ways in owning a gaming hell, you are an earl and future duke. I will not allow anyone to belittle you because your father was too stupid to see sense and reason. And your mama will help ensure your future," she explained.

"How so?" Grady asked, curious. "Mother has not been in society since before my birth."

"She is going to reenter society and take up her position as Duchess of Blackhaven. After all, it is her name, and she will no longer allow her husband to be the foolish man he has been to date. She will fight for you and us, and I love her for that as much as I love you. So very much," she said, her eyes glistening in the candlelight.

Grady leaned down and took her lips, drinking from them like a man starved of water. She was soft and as sweet as he remembered. The salty taste of her tears mingled with their kiss. He scooped her up into his arms and walked her to the nearby daybed, laying her down on the cool silk cushions.

Grady made light work of her clothing. Stripping her of her gown much faster than her masculine attire. She lay before him, a delicious naked feast for his eyes only. For his mouth and hands exclusively.

Her eyes greedily watched as he pulled his shirt over his head, kicking off his boots and breeches and tossing them onto the floor.

He liked having her eyes on him. He never wanted anyone else other than the woman willing and waiting for his touch.

He came over her, lifting her legs to straddle his waist, and took her in one hard thrust. She gasped his name, throwing her head back in ecstasy. Grady kissed her neck, her chest, her breasts, reveling in her warmth and wantonness as he made love to her.

His body roared for release, to claim her as his, but he held back. Wanting her to peak, to reach climax. Her ride to euphoria made his all the sweeter.

"Grady," she gasped. She tightened her legs and pushed at his chest, flipping him onto his back.

He lay back, determined to enjoy the view. What a marvelous woman she was. Fiery and bold. Loving and kind. He did not think his heart could love her any more than it did right now. So full of emotion it could burst.

"You're a minx. I knew it from the first moment we met that you would be trouble."

She rode him, her fingers on his chest, scoring his skin. She moaned, rolling her hips in a way that made his balls tighten. He swallowed, fighting to control himself, not wanting to look like a green lad unable to please his partner.

"You like that I am," she said. All true, of course. He did like it. It was one of the reasons he agreed to help her in her quests. Merely to be with her, to have her at his reach whenever he could.

"I do like it," he said, clasping her hips and thrusting into her. She threw back her head, her long, brown locks sliding over her shoulders. Her breasts rocked with each downward stroke, and he knew he was close. Watching her, enjoying her enjoy him, he knew it was too much.

"You're going to make me come, love."

She chuckled, a deep seductive sound that went straight to his cock. "Not yet, you're not," she said, slipping off him. "We haven't finished yet, my love. This is just the beginning."

# CHAPTER
# TWENTY-SIX

The sight of Grady beneath her, naked and hers to do with as she wished, sent a power of evocative delight running through her. She maneuvered her hands over his chest, enjoying the tickling sensation of the scattering of hair beneath her palms as it slipped through her fingers.

His stomach tightened and rose with each breath, and his manhood jutted up, glistening in the candlelight.

She had never seen a penis as close as she was to Grady's right at this moment. It was long and wide, fine blue veins running along its shaft. She wanted to touch him and play with him as he had so often done to her.

He watched her, the wicked dare in his green eyes making her bold. She clasped him firmly, sliding her hand along his length, mimicking how she rode him only moments before.

He closed his eyes. His intake of breath and following moan told her all that she needed to know. He enjoyed her touch, and by his thrust into her hand, he wanted more of the same.

She kneeled at his side, positioning herself to give him what he wanted, what she wanted too. To bring him enjoyment, pleasure like he so often gave her, was what life was made for. She wanted to please and be pleased, and this marvelous penis in her hand had given her so much pleasure that she wanted to repay the favor.

A little bead of liquid sat at his tip before rolling down his shaft, helping to lubricate her hand. Without thought, Ashley dipped her head and licked the end of his cock.

"God damn it, Ashley," he moaned. "You undo me." He gasped, biting his lip and watching her through hooded eyes.

"You undo me all the time. It is only fair to repay the favor," she said, repeatedly dipping her head.

This time, she went further, taking his manhood into her mouth, sliding it farther down her throat as she tried to accept him fully. He was large, and the action was not easy, but she wanted to give him all she could.

He groaned, his hands fisting into the cushions as she worked him with her mouth. With each stroke of her tongue, with each suckle of her lips, he grew harder. Pushed a little farther into her mouth.

His hands clasped her head, guiding her, holding her upon him, and wetness pooled at her core. She wanted his mouth on her. She wanted this marvelous cock in her cunny.

He had made her a wanton woman, and she loved that he did. That only with him did she want this.

She moaned, sucking him hard, teasing him with her tongue. He tasted delicious, salty, and hers.

All hers.

Forever.

Ashley sucked harder and tried to increase her pace.

Grady sat up, pulled her from his cock, and wrenched her onto his lap. She straddled him, lowering her aching cunny onto his cock.

He was so hard. He filled her and teased her from within, which always drove her to distraction.

She rode him, and he helped her. Their mouths crashed together, his tongue tangling with hers. This was no slow, seductive kiss. This kiss was full of passion, heat, and demands that they both would meet.

On it went. He took her as she took him in a fiery tangle of desire.

"Marry me," he asked her, meeting her eye.

Her lips lifted in a slow grin, and she halted her movements, tangling her fingers into the hair at the nape of his neck. "Marry you? I may have to think about it," she teased.

He thrust into her, and she groaned, wanting him to do that again. "Yes, very well. I will marry you, my darling love. Since you asked me so very nicely."

Ashley squealed when he lifted her from his lap and set her on her knees. He kneeled behind her, running his cock over her sex but not entering her.

She pushed back on him, wanting him in her. "Don't tease me, Grady," she begged, knowing she would do a lot more of that if he did not take her soon.

"You're so beautiful. I do not deserve you," he said, pressing the tip of his cock into her but not going any farther.

The annoying man was trying to drive her insane! "You do deserve me as I deserve you. We're made for each other, and if you entered me, well, you would even see that we're made to fit each other perfectly."

He chuckled but did not say a word.

Ashley wiggled back, moaning as his cock slipped a little farther inside.

Yes, this is what she wanted.

Him.

Grady.

His hands tightened on her ass, and he thrust into her, repeatedly, with hard, delicious pumps that taunted her cunny. She panted his name, throwing her head back as he took her without heed.

"Yes, Grady," she screamed as the first contractions of her delectable release spasmed from her core, out through her body in satisfying waves.

His pace never changed, and she felt his cock swell before he, too, found his release. He gasped her name, pumping his seed into her body without heed. Promising her everything he had, the world, and more.

She rode out her climax and hoped that his seed took root. That out of their love, their lovemaking, a little piece of them both would be created.

A future, a family, that was theirs.

Together.

# EPILOGUE

*1809 Blackhaven Estate, Surrey*

A grin lifted Ashley's lips as she cantered toward her home in Surrey with Grady as he waited near the stables for her return. They had been married almost eight months, and the Season of 1809 was about to begin.

They had decided to throw a week-long house party to kick off the Season and had invited all her family and their friends to the Blackhaven Estate.

She slid from the horse into Grady's arms. She wrapped hers around his neck, kissing him before their stable staff without caring who saw them.

"Did you miss me, darling?" she asked him, laughing when he pulled her closer still.

"Always, but I have come to collect you. Millie is arguing with Romney again."

Ashley sighed, fighting the urge to roll her eyes. "They argued yesterday over cook's kippers at breakfast. What are they arguing about now?" she asked. Surely there wasn't that much to row with someone about. She was almost at her wit's end with her sister, who looked to be a handful during the next Season. Something that her siblings had placed into her responsibility as her sponsor.

"They're arguing over which horse won the 1805 Kiplingcotes Derby. It is an absurd argument, but both are not backing down, and I think your mother will need smelling salts soon if they're not separated."

"Oh dear," Ashley said, increasing her pace toward the house. "How else is the house party going? Has your father been behaving himself?" she asked.

"So far," Grady said, his voice a little unsure.

Ashley glanced at him but did not get a chance to question him further, for as soon as they entered the house, she could hear Millie and Romney arguing in the front parlor where everyone congregated after breakfast.

They entered the room, and Millie gestured toward Ashley and Grady. "Ah, here you are. Please tell the duke that he has no idea about women's fashion. He is trying to tell me that *La Belle Assemblée* is not at the forefront of what women should read if they wish to keep abreast of women's fashion. He thinks," she said, glaring at the duke and receiving one back in return, "that a lady ought to be reading the *Lady's Magazine*. How absurd is that? Tell him, Ashley, that he is wrong, and he needs to stop putting his opinions on things that have nothing to do with him."

"I protest. I think women's fashion has everything to do with me." Romney smirked.

Millie laughed, the sound unamused. "How hilarious you are. But do tell us why, Your Grace. I did not take you for a man who needed to know what you should wear for a ball or dinner. Pray tell me, what pretty gown will you have on this evening, I wonder." Millie mocked.

A dark blush kissed Romney's cheeks before he stood and strode from the room. Millie looked after him as if she had just conquered a beast in a superfine coat.

"That is enough, Millie. You cannot be so rude," Ashley chastised. "Even if you are correct. *La Belle Assemblée* is the magazine one needs to read."

Grady groaned before they took their seats. Most of the family were here already, except Viscount and Viscountess Leigh, who would be arriving tomorrow.

Derby and Chilsten and her sisters Hailey and Julia sat talking to their mama. Her sister Hailey having not long started her family and birthed a healthy baby boy. Derby looked on, cooing over the newest member of their family with so much pride and love that Ashley couldn't help but get a lump in her throat.

"I want that for you too, my love. And one day, it will happen. Do not get despondent," Grady said, knowing how much Ashley wanted a child with him. It had not happened yet, but he was right. One day they would be blessed.

"How are your mama and Blackhaven getting on?" she asked Grady.

After their wedding in London, the duchess, true to her word, had set about reentering society. And while doing so seemed to have found a backbone that the duke had not been expecting.

And somehow, in the whirlwind of their wedding and moving into a delightful town house on Berkeley Square so she could be near Hailey, the estranged duke and duchess had formed a peace of sorts.

"Have a look for yourself. They are over at the pianoforte, working out what music will be played this evening."

Ashley studied the pair and did not miss how the

duchess looked at the duke and His Grace at her in return. There was still love there, and perhaps now that he agreed Grady was his, that he was indeed too much like him in looks not to be, there could still be a future for them. Even after all this time.

"Your mama looks happy, my love. But what about you? How do you feel about what is happening between them?" she asked Grady.

His eyes narrowed, and he shrugged. "I do not know what I feel about it. I'm happy for her, but he abandoned us for so long. Let people talk of us as if we were scum. That is not so easy to forgive and forget."

Ashley clasped his jaw, turning him to face her. "You do not have to forgive or forget anything that caused you pain."

He leaned toward her and kissed her, something he often did, no matter who was about them.

"Have I told you today how much I adore and love you?" he asked her.

She grinned, shuffling in close to him. He wrapped his arm around her and held her close. "Yes, this morning, if you remember?" she said.

A wicked light entered his eyes, and he waggled his brows at her. "Shall we return upstairs so I may tell you again? In private?"

"Your library is closer."

"My father's library, you mean," he said.

Ashley shook her head. "This house is ours now, remember? He's moved into the dowager house with the duchess. So that means the library is now yours to use at your will."

Another wonderous change of heart that she knew Grady was struggling with. That his father, although still the Duke of Blackhaven, had taken a step back from running the estates and had handed over everything to his son, all but the title. Ashley knew that Grady's mama had everything to do with the cold, heartless duke's change of opinion and manners. And she could not help but feel for the duke a little. The man was desperate to win back his son's love, but Ashley did not know if it would ever happen. And she would not force Grady into anything he did not want to do.

"That is very true... And we never did get to finish what we started at Whites. Shall we excuse ourselves for a moment?"

Ashley stood without another word and headed for the door. The sound of her husband's hurried footsteps behind her made her smile, and by the time they crossed the hall to the library, they were both laughing.

He was as wicked as he was the night she met him, and her heart could not be more full.

G rady bundled Ashley into the library and closed the door, snicking the lock to ensure they were alone and that it remained that way.

He stalked her across the room until her delectable ass bumped against the desk.

He hoisted her onto the red, shining mahogany and made short work of her rich blue riding habit that she was yet to change out of. It pooled at her waist, and he settled between her thighs, her warmth, the scent of her need making his mouth water.

"I always want you," he whispered against her ear, eliciting a shiver through her body.

Her fingers tangled into his hair, pulling him to her. "I am the same."

Grady ripped his falls open, his cock springing into his hand. They had not been able to do this at Whites. They had been interrupted, and his balls had been blue for days until he had finally had Ashley in truth.

He slid into her heat, her legs pinning him against her. She was so tight, hot, and his. She gasped and kissed him with a wantonness that left him mindless with need.

After all these months as her husband, still, she drove him to distraction. He could not live without her. Without her love and sunshine.

"You're so beautiful. I love you so much," he gasped against her lips.

She chuckled through their kiss, her tongue tangling with his. His balls hardened, and his cock ached to spend. She tilted her hips, taking him deeper, and all coherent thoughts vanished.

"Fuck me, Grady," she said, her filthy talk pushing him to the brink.

He did as she asked. Heedless of how loud they were, he gave her all that she wanted, pushed her, thrust into her with maddening strokes. A quill, a book, and parchment fell to the floor, and he was ignorant of it all.

He was consumed by the need to make her shatter.

The first quiverings of her cunny drew at his cock, and she gasped his name, pulling him against her as she rode her orgasm to completion. His name on her lips muffled against his shoulder. Grady followed her, spent himself to utter rapture in her arms. They stayed at the desk for several minutes, joined and holding the other as they caught their breath.

"Maybe we ought to sneak into Whites one day as we

once did and complete our excursion. I must admit, the desk is a marvelous invention for such couplings."

He shook his head, laughing at their antics, which had been many since they married. "You're trouble, just as I said you were."

"And you're my trouble, just as I knew you always would be."

That he was. Always and forever.

*Mine.*

Hers.

His.

Dear Reader,

Thank you for taking the time to read *Every Duke has a Silver Lining*! I hope you enjoyed the fourth book in my Wayward Woodvilles series!

I'm so thankful for my readers support. If you're able, I would appreciate an honest review of *Every Duke has a Silver Lining*. As they say, feed an author, leave a review!

Alternatively, you can keep in contact with me by visiting my website, subscribing to my newsletter or following me online. You can contact me at www.-tamaragill.com.

Tamara Gill

# THE WAYWARD WOODVILLES

Series starts Feb, 2022
Pre-order your copy today!

# DON'T MISS TAMARA'S OTHER ROMANCE SERIES

## The Wayward Woodvilles

A Duke of a Time

On a Wild Duke Chase

Speak of the Duke

Every Duke has a Silver Lining

One Day my Duke will Come

Surrender to the Duke

My Reckless Earl

Brazen Rogue

The Notorious Lord Sin

Wicked in My Bed

## Royal House of Atharia

To Dream of You

A Royal Proposition

Forever My Princess

## League of Unweddable Gentlemen

Tempt Me, Your Grace

Hellion at Heart

Dare to be Scandalous

To Be Wicked With You

Kiss Me, Duke

The Marquess is Mine

**Kiss the Wallflower**

A Midsummer Kiss

A Kiss at Mistletoe

A Kiss in Spring

To Fall For a Kiss

A Duke's Wild Kiss

To Kiss a Highland Rose

**Lords of London**

To Bedevil a Duke

To Madden a Marquess

To Tempt an Earl

To Vex a Viscount

To Dare a Duchess

To Marry a Marchioness

**To Marry a Rogue**

Only an Earl Will Do

Only a Duke Will Do

Only a Viscount Will Do

Only a Marquess Will Do

Only a Lady Will Do

**A Time Traveler's Highland Love**

To Conquer a Scot

To Save a Savage Scot

To Win a Highland Scot

**A Stolen Season**

A Stolen Season

A Stolen Season: Bath

A Stolen Season: London

**Scandalous London**

A Gentleman's Promise

A Captain's Order

A Marriage Made in Mayfair

**High Seas & High Stakes**

His Lady Smuggler

Her Gentleman Pirate

**Daughters Of The Gods**

Banished

Guardian

Fallen

**Stand Alone Books**

Defiant Surrender

A Brazen Agreement

To Sin with Scandal

Outlaws

# About the Author

Tamara is an Australian author who grew up in an old mining town in country South Australia, where her love of history was founded. So much so, she made her darling husband travel to the UK for their honeymoon, where she dragged him from one historical monument and castle to another.

A mother of three, her two little gentlemen in the making, a future lady (she hopes) keep her busy in the real world, but whenever she gets a moment's peace she loves to write romance novels in an array of genres, including regency, medieval and time travel.

Made in the USA
Las Vegas, NV
07 July 2023

74332896R00098